THE LEGEND OF
ANDREW RUFUS
BOOK 1
DARK AWAKENING

For my boys...always.
And, the ether.
Thank you.

D1713871

Author: Crumley, M.M.
Title: THE LEGEND OF ANDREW RUFUS: DARK AWAKENING
Series: The Legend of Andrew Rufus; 1.
Target Audience: Ages fourteen though adult

Subjects: Apprentices-fiction/ Fantasy/ Juvenile Fiction/ Action & Adventure/
Survival Stories / Legends, Myths, Fables, Lore, Hero's/ Fantasy & Magic/
General Awesomeness and All Things Epic.

Also available in this series
THE LEGEND OF ANDREW RUFUS: BONE DEEP (Book 2)
THE LEGEND OF ANDREW RUFUS: BLOOD STAINED (Book 3)
THE LEGEND OF ANDREW RUFUS: BURIAL GROUND (Book 4)
THE LEGEND OF ANDREW RUFUS: DEATH SONG (Book 5)
THE LEGEND OF ANDREW RUFUS: FUNERAL MARCH (Book 6)
THE LEGEND OF ANDREW RUFUS: WARPATH (Book 7)

THE LEGEND OF
ANDREW RUFUS
BOOK 1
DARK AWAKENING

M.M. Crumley

LONE GHOST
Publishing

Never Give Up The Ghost

A Special Note to My Young Readers

When I was a kid I read a ton of books, and many of them came from my much older brother. Some of them I wasn't ready for yet. Some I'll never be ready for! But I read them anyway. Maybe I thought I'd be a wussy if I didn't finish; I don't know. It took me years to learn that if I'm uncomfortable with a book I need to stop reading. Even now, at my ripe old age, I sometimes put a book down.

You're the only one who knows whether or not you're ready for a book (or a show or a movie). Pretend you're reading a book that all your friends are saying is "amazing and awesome and the best book ever", but you don't like it. Maybe it scares you, maybe it makes you uncomfortable, maybe you just don't like the writing. PUT IT DOWN!!! Even if it's my book. It doesn't make you a wussy; it makes you brave and individual and wise. You'll know when you're ready.

Happy Reading!

M.M. Crumley

Read all the Adventures of
ANDREW RUFUS

Prologue

There are places, hidden places, where it seems time does not exist. But this cannot be true. Time exists, in all things, in all places; it is connected, interwoven, set, and unchangeable... Except that it isn't. A nudge here, a tug there...

Time should never be meddled with. It is far too delicate, too precious, too unknown. The ripples from even the smallest change go on forever and ever and ever. That is why, when one IS meddling with the fabric of time, one must do so very, very carefully.

Chapter One

Andrew Rufus jolted as the earth shifted beneath him. He tightened his hands and legs in reactive fear, and his heart nearly stuttered to a stop as he realized he was straddling a horse. He blinked wildly in confusion, then looked down and gasped. It wasn't him. He was seeing out of someone else's eyes; those weren't his hands or his arms he was looking at. Those weren't his legs. Everything was wrong. He looked out past those terribly strange hands, and his stomach tensed. The scenery was zipping past, just a blur of motion. It was too fast. If he didn't stop he was going to be sick.

The horse suddenly leaped into the air, and Andrew jerked in terror, grasping the horse's mane tightly. The horse landed with a thud and tossed its head wildly.

"Oh crap!" Andrew cried out as he began to fall. He flung his arms around the horse's neck and held on for dear life, desperately hoping the horse would stop.

Then he heard it. An angry voice, gruff and gravely, yelling, yelling very loudly, INSIDE Andrew's head.

WHAT THE HELL'S GOIN' ON?!

Andrew screamed; he screamed at the top of his lungs. He screamed, plugged his ears, and closed his eyes, hoping when he opened them again he'd be back in his room. But the more he screamed the more the voice inside his head yelled.

*WHAT THE HELL YOU DOIN'?! STOP THAT
SISSY CRYIN'! RIGHT NOW!!!*

The horse had stopped running, which was good
since Andrew's hands were covering his ears, but he
didn't know how to get off it. He was so high up, and
the ground was so far down; it made his head spin. His
mind raced, trying to figure out what was going on, but
he simply couldn't think. The voice in his head was too
loud. Why was there a voice in his head? Where was
his body? Where was he? What was happening?

Who are you?! the voice snapped. *You some kinda
witch?*

"Witch? What? No," Andrew stuttered, eyes
widening when he heard his voice. It didn't sound right
at all. It was deep and menacing, like the voice in his
head. He stared at his hands again. They moved when
he moved them, but they weren't his hands. The wide,
red gash from his fall wasn't there. These hands had
thin, white scars across the knuckles; they were
callused, sun-browned, and huge, full-grown.

Andrew squeezed his eyes shut. He must have
fallen asleep reading that stupid book, and now he was
dreaming. That's what was happening. He was
dreaming. All he had to do was wake up. He pinched
himself. It hurt, but he didn't wake. He slapped
himself. Tears welled in his eyes it stung so badly, but
he still didn't wake up.

What the hell you doin'?!

"Trying to wake up," Andrew mumbled, weirded
out he was having a conversation with someone he

couldn't see. Like he was talking to himself, but he wasn't. It felt like madness.

Wake up?

"I'm asleep; that's the only explanation."

Asleep? I ain't asleep. GET THE HELL OUT OF MY BODY!! NOW!

"I don't know how." Andrew glanced around. This was surely the most vivid dream he'd ever had. It was so vivid he could feel the heat and taste the dirt. Maybe he should back off the painkillers. His broken leg didn't really hurt all that much anymore.

Try! the voice snapped.

"How? I don't know how I got in here." Andrew was trying to remember if he'd ever had a conversation in a dream before, but the voice just wouldn't shut up.

GET OUT!!!

"I already told you, I can't!"

Do it anyway!

"How?"

Just do!

Andrew rolled his eyes. "It's just a dream, you know. I'm sure I'll wake up soon, and then you'll have your body back." What a dorky thing to say. When he woke up, the dream would be gone. He wasn't so scared now that he realized it was a dream. He was sure he could ride a horse in a dream, and if he fell, he'd just wake up.

When I get my hands on you, I'm gonna tie you in a knot.

"A knot?" Andrew laughed. "Is that really the best you've got?"

You laughin' at me?

"A little. Be pretty hard to tie someone into a knot. Beat me up, sure. Tie into a knot? I don't know."

Who the hell are you?!

This was bizarre, but his mom hated it when he was rude, so Andrew sighed and said, "Andrew Rufus; and you?"

Pecos Bill.

Andrew burst out laughing. Now he was certain it was a dream. He felt stupid for not realizing it right away; everything had just felt so real. The sun was burning down on his back; he could feel the horse's sides moving under his legs; he could feel the roughness of its hair beneath his hands. He'd never had such an intense dream before. It was so real, so vibrant. It had to be the drugs.

What's so funny? Pecos snapped.

"Nothing, it's just…I really am dreaming."

What the hell you talkin' 'bout?! Ain't no dream! What'd you say your name was? Andrew, Andrew Rufus, Andrew thought, wondering if he needed to speak out loud for Pecos to hear him. *Ain't never heard of you,* Pecos growled back. Course not. You're not real. I'm real. I'm dreaming, so I've heard of you 'cause you're in that dumb book I was reading before I fell asleep. *What?!*

Andrew sighed. Dreams weren't usually so complicated. When he woke up, he was tossing the pills in the trash. Listen, I'm not really here. You're not really here. This is all just a dream. *Ain't no damn dream!* Pecos sputtered. *Get out of my body right this minute...*

Pecos went on and on, but Andrew wasn't listening because he'd just noticed three other riders heading towards him. They were already fairly close, and Andrew could just make out their faces. He was glad he was dreaming because he didn't know how to make the horse go again, and if this were real life, he'd be riding the other way. He'd never seen such scary looking dudes.

They had serious expressions on their faces and guns on their hips. Lots and lots of guns. And knives. They were riding into the sun, so their faces were shining, and a shudder ran down Andrew's spine when his eyes locked onto one of the men.

"Somethin' wrong, Pecos?" the man asked as they stopped their horses beside Andrew.

Andrew gulped. "Um...I..." He didn't go on, just stared at the man in horror.

He had a stone-hard face, brilliant, blue eyes, and a scar running from his nose to his ear. His tight blond goatee was broken in the middle by another scar. There were a ridiculous amount of guns strapped all over him, maybe six or eight, and Andrew was certain he didn't have any problem using them.

Andrew tore his eyes away and looked at one of the other men. He instantly regretted it. These dudes were so creepy Andrew wished he could wake up. He'd never be mean to his mom again. He'd tell her he loved her, because he did. He'd promise to never climb a tree ever again. He'd keep both feet on the ground, and he'd swear off painkillers for the rest of his life.

The second man wasn't wearing a hat, and his skin was as dark as the surrounding dirt, maybe darker. His hair was loose, flowing down his back in a shimmery, black wave, and Andrew guessed he was Native American, but he wasn't sure. His dark eyes were unfathomable, unreadable, but the worst part was that in addition to a bow and a few guns, he was wearing so many knives Andrew didn't even try to count them.

Andrew shuddered, wondering what Pecos must look like if these were the type of guys he hung out with, and glanced at the third man. He actually looked normal enough except he had the widest and curliest mustache Andrew had ever seen. His eyes were a laughing brown, and his lips were curved in a slight grin. He seemed to be wearing a normal amount of weapons, but Andrew couldn't be sure. He'd never been around anyone who carried a gun or a knife before, let alone eight of them. He wasn't sure how he'd imagined these guys; he was positive the book hadn't been all that descriptive.

"Pecos?" the blond man asked again, a thread of annoyance in his tone.

Listen you coward, you body thief! Pecos was yelling. *Get out of my body right this damn minute or I'm gonna truss you up and leave you for the coyotes!* How's that better than a knot? I mean, how're you gonna do it?

Pecos growled, and Andrew glanced between the three men, feeling trapped, like the time Chuck had pulled a prank on Principal Banks, but Andrew had been caught holding the spray can.

He opened his mouth to reply to the blond man, but Pecos started yelling again, so loud Andrew flinched. Shut up so I can think! Andrew snapped. *Shut up?! Shut up?! This is my body! You shut up, damn it!* Right now it's my body! So you shut up! *You ain't no man, just a coward!*

I'm not a coward or a man! Andrew thought angrily. His head was starting to ache. There was just too much going on. Could your head even ache in a dream? I'm only thirteen, Andrew added. And I didn't steal your stupid body; why would I even want to? I just kinda ended up here. And it doesn't matter, 'cause THIS IS A DREAM!!!

This was getting weirder and weirder by the second. He'd pay good money for his mom to wake him and tussle his hair. She could call him "baby" and sit by his bed all day asking him how he was, and he wouldn't even care.

Pecos started yelling again, but Andrew tried to ignore him because the mustached man was talking.

"You alright, Pecos?"

"Um…yeah, just thinking."

"Thinkin' 'bout what?" the blond man snapped.

Andrew cringed. The blond guy freaked him out. He looked like the kind of guy who shot first and didn't bother to ask questions, ever. "I don't know…Just thinking."

The knife man had been watching Andrew or Pecos, whoever he was, intently, but now he spoke. "You wantin' to change your plan?"

Andrew grabbed at that. "Plan? What plan exactly?"

The blond man frowned deeply, but the knife man smiled slightly and replied, "The one you just made."

Andrew sighed; that had really cleared things up. "Let me think about it," he stalled. Help me out here, Pecos? *Ain't helpin' you, boy! You need to disappear.* I really wish I could, but I can't. I've never tried to wake up in a dream before; I don't know how to do it. *I done told you boy, ain't no dream,* Pecos said in a weary tone. Of course it is, but I still don't wanna get shot to death by your gun-happy friends. They'd like an answer, and I don't have any idea what they're talking about.

Ain't gonna shoot me. No, but they might shoot me, and see, I'm in your body in the middle of...of... Andrew looked around. There was nothing as far as he could see except dirt and rocks and little scrubby plants and what he assumed were cactus clumps. He'd never seen actual cactuses before. There were so many of them.

Why are we in a desert? *Ain't a desert, boy. Just a bit of dry land is all. We ridin' to stop the snake.* Andrew accidentally laughed. "Sorry," he said quickly. "Just thought of something funny. Still thinking," he added when the blond man opened his mouth to speak.

Four guys to stop one measly snake? You're kidding me right? You're supposed to be a western legend! You fight things like tornados and rustlers and blue cows or something, right? *Watch it, boy...* Or what?

Andrew was beginning to enjoy himself. He hadn't had any fun in days; not since that stupid, wild, grey cat had knocked him out of the tree. Sure the cowboy dudes were scary looking; but it was a dream, and as such, nothing really bad could happen. And if it did, he'd just wake up. Like that one dream where he'd showed up to school naked. He'd woken just as the bell rang right before everyone filed out into the hall and laughed at him.

This ain't a dream or a pleasure trip or a damn party! If you don't get outta my body right now folks're gonna die! Andrew rolled his eyes. What did it matter if people died in a dream? It's not like they were real. *THIS IS REAL!!! Can't you feel it?!*

Andrew shook his head, annoyed Pecos was so serious. It's too bad he hadn't had a baseball dream instead. One with Willie Mays and Derek Jeter and Babe Ruth. Andrew would pitch and see if they could get a hit. Now that would have been fun.

The only thing I can feel is the sun, Andrew complained. Is it always this hot? *That's just it, boy. When's the last time you felt the sun in a dream?* Andrew chose not to think about that. It was weird that he was so hot, that he was sweating, that he could feel the breeze cooling him down, but there was an explanation for that. His pain pills clearly had some terrible side effects. They were probably experimental. He shuddered, wondering what else they were doing to him.

I can't believe this, Pecos sighed. *You've gotta be the densest boy on earth.* Andrew frowned. I'm not dense! If I believed you, a figment of my imagination I might add, THEN I would be dense! *Fine, just keep on ignorin' your senses, and while you do, people'll die. Thanks to you.*

Whatever, let's get back to the plan. You're riding to stop a snake. Is that the whole plan? *Yep.* Andrew rolled his eyes. Great plan, super involved, covers all the fine points. *Boy...* "I'm good," Andrew said out loud. "Um, lead the way somebody." He figured it couldn't hurt to play along until he woke up. It was certainly better than counting the stars on his ceiling. Again.

The blond man glared at him, but knife man nodded, turning his horse and riding away. The other two followed him, and Andrew sat, watching them. Um, how do I make the horse go? *Not THE horse; her name's Dewmint.* Okay, how do I make Dewmint go? Pecos sighed. *Pick up the reins, tap with your heels, nice like.* Reins? *The leather straps,* Pecos ground out. Oh. Andrew picked up the reins and tapped with his heels.

Dewmint started walking, and Andrew gasped, clutching her mane with his hands. *What you doin'?* Trying not to fall off! *Ain't you never ridden before?* I've never even touched a horse before, let alone ridden one! Andrew was suddenly very aware how far away the ground was. Are all horses this tall? *Dewmint ain't that tall, just sixteen hands.* Hands? Pretty sure we measure in feet. *Boy...* Never mind; how do I go faster?

Andrew didn't actually want to go faster, but the others were far ahead of him, and he figured he should probably catch up. Dream or no dream, he didn't want to get left behind in the desert or really dry landscape as Pecos called it. *Heels.* Oh. Andrew tapped his heels again, and Dewmint sped up.

Andrew closed his eyes in fear. But that was even worse, so he opened them again. This is stupid, he thought. Why am I scared? It's a dream! A super realistic dream, but a dream. *Never seen such an idiot in all my days, and that's sayin' somethin'.* Oh, shut up, Andrew snapped. You don't exist, and even if you did, which you don't, it's not possible to take over someone else's body. It's just not. That kinda crap doesn't even happen in movies. You know why? 'Cause no one would believe it!

Andrew tried to relax as Dewmint moved across the ground. He was still far behind the others, so he nudged her again. She sped up, and Andrew clutched the reins in terror. She was going so fast, and everything was so bouncy, he felt like his back was breaking. He clenched his jaw to keep his teeth from clanking together with every step the horse took. *Downright embarrassin'. Of all the body thieves, I get a sissy, city slicker boy.*

Excuse me! I'm not a sissy or a…well, I guess I am a city slicker and a boy, but I'm not a sissy! So you take that back! *Ain't takin' nothin' back. What the hell you doin' here?* I told you already! I'M DREAMING!!! So stop asking!

If Pecos would just shut up, this could be the most epic dream ever. He was riding a horse, something his mom would never let him do; he was outside, instead of stuck in his room with a busted leg and no TV, riding through a landscape he'd never seen before; and he had guns, and they were probably loaded. *Don't you dare touch my guns, boy!* Can't stop me, Andrew thought laughingly.

He tried to look around, but it was hard because when he took his eyes off Dewmint's head, he felt like he was falling. But when he managed to look right for a second, he realized there were two more horses running behind him, reins attached to his saddle. He looked forward again and saw the others had extra horses too. Why do you have so many horses? *Ridin' hard.* So? *If you weren't a city slicker you would know!* Whatever.

Andrew glanced over Dewmint's head and saw waves of heat rolling off the dirt into the air. He'd never been able to see so far in all his life. He'd always been surrounded by buildings or trees. It felt so empty. He wondered if the desert really looked like this. He didn't think he'd seen many pictures of the desert, so he wasn't sure what his mind was basing this on. He heard Pecos sigh. *Ain't a dream, boy. It's real; as real as the nose on your, I mean MY, face.* Andrew shook his head. It's not real! It's a dream. But since you're clearly not gonna shut up, tell me more about your plan.

Dewmint was going really fast now, and Andrew was having a horrible time sitting upright. He kept sliding from side to side and having to wiggle back into the middle of the saddle. *Relax your back,* Pecos chided. Andrew tried, but every time Dewmint's hooves hit the ground, he jerked.

No wonder people don't ride horses anymore, he thought as he dragged himself upright. *Whadda you mean people don't ride horses?* Can you hear everything I think? *Mostly.* Well stop! It's annoying. *Whadda you mean?* Where I'm from, or when I'm from I guess, people drive cars and trucks and stuff. *Cars?* Like a...a wagon that doesn't need horses. Andrew shook his head with irritation. Why was he explaining this? It didn't matter if Pecos knew what a car was. He was going to disappear as soon as Andrew woke up. Andrew pinched himself just to check, but he stayed right where he was.

He frowned, looking around in confusion. Everything was super, super real. The details of the landscape, Dewmint's mane, the heat of the sun, the smell of dust, the thirst in his throat, the ache in his rear, the voice in his head. All of it FELT real. But that would mean...he shook his head emphatically. Why was he even considering it?

Snake, Pecos? What about the snake? Pecos chuckled softly. *You ain't gonna like the snake, boy.*

Chapter Two

I have a name you know, Andrew thought irritably. It's Andrew. Pecos didn't respond, but Andrew didn't really care. As soon as he woke up he was dumping his pain pills and that stupid book in the trashcan. This was the worst dream ever. For a moment there he'd thought it was going to be fun, an escape from his bad day, but it was turning out to be even worse than being bored in his room all alone with nothing to do.

For one, it was hot. Like boiling hot. For two, riding a horse was painful. Like really painful. For three, Pecos was not a fun headmate. Like a roommate, but in Andrew's head. Andrew frowned. Head neighbor? Mind neighbor? Mindmate? Nah, headmate sounded best.

Dewmint was running over the rocks and occasionally jumping over little bushes making Andrew's heart leap into his throat. And every time her hooves hit the ground, Andrew jerked, and when he jerked, it hurt. A lot. But that wasn't the worst of it; the worst of it was he was starting to need to pee.

He couldn't remember ever having to pee in a dream before, and he was trying to decide if needing to pee in a dream meant he had to pee in real life, and if that was the case why didn't he just wake up? After an excruciatingly long time of bouncing with no apparent end in sight, Andrew finally asked, Are we almost there?

Have to ask Charlie. Pecos had been silent until now, and Andrew jumped when he spoke. It was freaky having someone else's voice in his head. Which one's Charlie? *He ain't wearin' a hat.* Oh. Who's the one with the mustache? *Joe.* And the creepy guy? *Doyle? He ain't creepy.* Is too, Andrew thought with a shudder.

Where're we going? *To fight the snake.* What snake? Where is it? And why're you fighting it? *Needs done.* That didn't tell Andrew a thing. So do you think it'll be much longer? *I done told you, have to ask Charlie.* I don't wanna ask Charlie. *Then we'll get there when we get there* Pecos growled. That doesn't work for me. *Boy, this ain't some fun shindig! We got work to do!*

Andrew felt heat flood his face. He didn't want to tell Pecos, but he couldn't see any way around it. It was like having to raise his hand in class to ask to use the bathroom. It was embarrassing, and Pecos already thought he was a sissy.

I need to pee, okay? he thought with a sigh. Really, really need to pee. The horse is bouncing up and down, and… *Why didn't you just say so?* 'Cause I don't wanna pee! I'm not gonna pee, 'cause if I pee here what if I pee there? And anyway, I'm not in my body, I'm in yours. And I am NOT peeing in your body! *Then why'd you bring it up?* 'Cause if we don't get there soon…well… *You control yourself, boy! If you disgrace my body...* Pecos growled something else, but it was so low, Andrew couldn't hear it.

Andrew wished he'd kept his mouth shut; he felt like an absolute idiot. He hated this dream. He hated Pecos, and he hated Chuck. This was all Chuck's fault. If it wasn't for Chuck and his big mouth, Andrew would be fishing right now.

Far ahead he could see the landscape was beginning to change, and he hoped that meant they'd be stopping soon. But they didn't. They rode and rode and rode. Andrew had no idea how long they rode, but it felt like hours. His bladder was screaming in agony, his hands were cramping, his legs felt like jelly, and he was sure his back was actually broken. At this rate, he'd never walk again. Not in this dream anyway.

They left the desert quite suddenly and were surrounded by short cedar-like trees. Before long, the others halted beside a ring of trees. Andrew was relieved when Dewmint stopped beside them. He looked around expectantly, but there was nothing to see. Just trees and more dirt. Certainly no snake, unless it was even smaller than most snakes.

Are we there? he asked. *Where?* Where we're going? *No.* Then why'd we stop? *Switch horses.* Switch horses? Why? *Just do it, boy.* What does that even mean? Pecos sighed. *Take the saddle off Dewmint,* he said very slowly. *Put it on Jiminty.* Okay, but why? *JUST DO IT!*

The others had already dismounted and were stripping their saddles from the horses they'd been riding. Andrew stared at the ground. It was a long way away. How do I get down? *Figure it out,* Pecos snapped. You're not being overly cooperative, Andrew snapped back. Maybe if he fell he'd wake up. He tried moving his leg over the horse's head as he'd seen the mustached man do, but he couldn't. He honestly couldn't feel his legs anymore. If he wasn't looking right at them, he'd think they'd fallen off.

Andrew finally dropped the reins and used his hands to lift his leg over the pointy saddle thingy. He yelped as he slid out of the saddle, foot twisting in the stirrup, and landed face first on the hard ground. He gasped, trying to regain his air, tears welling from the pain. He closed his eyes tightly and opened them cautiously expecting to see his familiar, star painted ceiling, but all he saw was red dirt and a lizard inches from his face.

Something was very, very wrong. He scrambled to his feet, wincing as the blood rushed back into his legs, to find the others staring at him openmouthed. He tried to smile, but Pecos's lips were too wide and his mouth so full of teeth, it felt wrong.

"Um...got a leg cramp, you know?" Andrew said shakily.

The one Pecos had called Charlie raised an eyebrow, but Doyle snarled, "Leg cramp?"

Andrew could hear Pecos groaning in disgust. "Just need to walk it off," Andrew muttered, turning and limping into the brush. He heard the low rumble of voices behind him, and he imagined they were wondering what the hell was wrong with Pecos.

His whole body hurt; but it wasn't his body. It didn't even feel like his body. The legs were super long, and every step he took felt heavy. Everything hurt so badly he just wanted to lie down on the dirt and die. He tried touching his toes, but he couldn't even reach them. *What you doin'?* Pecos growled. Trying to stretch. I'm so tight; everything hurts. *Quit it! You look ridiculous!* You can't even see me. *I can feel you, and you FEEL ridiculous! Quit it!* Andrew ignored Pecos and twisted side to side.

Shouldn't be stiff anyhow, Pecos grumbled. *I ain't never stiff.* Andrew rolled his eyes. I doubt that. *If you would just relax instead of sittin' like a poker in the saddle.* I'm trying, Andrew snapped. *You ride like a day-old corpse.* That's sick! *It's the truth!* Whatever.

Something trickled down his nose, and Andrew wiped his hand over it. His heart hammered wildly when he saw it wasn't sweat, but blood. "I'm bleeding," he said, jumping when he heard Pecos's voice saying his words. "But..." Andrew closed his eyes, then looked again. "I'm bleeding."

I'M bleeding, and it's 'cause you fell off my damn horse! You know how many times I've fallen off a horse? Andrew couldn't respond; his mind was blank with terror. *Never! That's how many. Not once!* "I'm bleeding," Andrew whispered.

He'd never bled in a dream. Not ever. He'd never hurt in a dream either. He'd won many a dream game by sliding into home plate, but it had never, ever hurt. And Andrew knew for a fact it hurt in real life. He'd even had a dream where a fish had bitten off his hand when he'd put it into a lake, but he hadn't bled. His hand had just been gone, and he hadn't felt a lick of pain.

Andrew dropped to the ground and stared at his hand. The blood was already turning brown, but it was blood, real blood, blood. He glanced around him. The sun was low in the sky, but the heat was still overpowering. Sweat ran down his back and neck. Something just wasn't right. He pinched his arm. It hurt, but he didn't wake up.

He had to be dreaming. He just had to. But he hurt; he hurt, and he bled, and damn it, he still needed to pee! Andrew stood and started pacing. His mom had been checking on him every fifteen minutes. Surely she would have come in by now. But if he was asleep she wouldn't have woken him, so that didn't help.

He'd been reading that book, that weird book about American Folklore that had smelled like Great-Grandpa Lester's tobacco smoke. He'd started with the story about Pecos Bill, the legendary cowboy hero, but he hadn't gotten very far. Could it have…no, he wasn't even going to finish that thought. He was dreaming, and that was the end of it. There was no other explanation.

Why not? Why not what? *Why can't there be another explanation?* Because there can't! *But why not? Can't you feel the stone beneath you?* Andrew could. He could feel everything. His breathing came faster and faster, and he tried to slow it, to breathe deeply.

He finally grasped at the one thing he could control. I really need to pee. *So? Do it!* Not with you watching! *What? That don't make no sense! It's my body.* I don't care! This is all so weird. I can't pee if you're watching, so close your eyes! *I can't you idiot.* Oh… Okay, I'll close my eyes. *Then how you gonna pee?* Who cares! I've gotta go!

Andrew stomped to a nearby bush, closed his eyes, hummed loudly, trying very hard not to think about what he was doing, and peed into the bush. The relief he felt was immense, and it terrified him. He wished he hadn't peed after all. It was too real. Everything was just too real. It was real. How the hell could it be real?!

You can't hide here forever. The others're gonna come lookin' for you. Andrew had forgotten about the others. He wasn't ready to see them. They were too big and too armed and too scary, and they were Pecos's men, so how scary was Pecos?

He tried to look at himself, but all he could see was the long blue sleeves covering his arms, the leather vest buttoned up his chest, the two belts of guns, the handles of two knives, and dusty brown pants, which were covered by some type of leather leggings. And the big pointy boots sticking out from underneath everything.

He put his hand on one of the gun handles just to see what it felt like. *Get your hand off that, boy!* Andrew jumped, pulling his hand away, but not before he'd felt the cool smoothness of the gun. He took the hat off his head and ran his fingertips along the edge. It was soft, but worn in places, and it was black underneath all the dust. The sun felt hot on his head, and he ran his hand through his hair. Pecos had thick, wavy hair similar to Andrew's own, but there was more of it.

Andrew shuddered, pushing the hat down on his head again. He didn't like this. He wanted out, and he wanted out now! Maybe if he yelled for his mom, she'd come wake him. "MOM!!!!" he yelled, voice louder than he'd expected. *WHAT THE HELL YOU DOIN?!* Pecos yelled just as loudly in his head.

Trying to wake up! Andrew snapped. *IT AIN'T A DREAM!* It has to be! "MOM!!!!" he screamed again. Andrew waited, but his mom didn't come. The sun merely dropped lower, and a light breeze began to blow.

Pecos sighed. *Look boy. I got work to do. And if you ain't gettin' out of my body then we're just gonna have to do it together.* Andrew fought the urge to curl into a ball and stay there until he woke. He was certain Pecos would yell at him until he got back up; if Doyle didn't shoot him first.

He didn't want to go; there was no point in going, but he couldn't stay here. It was hot, it was getting dark, and he didn't want to be all alone. And he was thirsty. Thirsty and hungry. How could he be thirsty? If he stayed here, he'd go crazy trying to work out what was happening. He was going to have to go with them. He was going to have to keep riding.

Okay, he sighed. Whadda I do? *Switch horses and ride.* Andrew walked as slowly as possible back towards the others, dreading what happened next, but when he got there, he saw his saddle was already on a different horse. The only reason he could tell was because this horse was even taller.

Don't you have any short horses? *These are the short ones. You should see Widow Maker. Bet he's twenty hands tall, but he won't stay still long enough to be measured.* Widow Maker? *Hell of a horse; faster than the wind.* Okay, but Widow Maker? What kinda name is that? Pecos snorted. *Come on city slicker; figure it out.* For real? What's this horse named?

Only someone certifiably insane would ride a horse named Widow Maker. Someone like Pecos. Andrew would never ride a horse named Widow Maker, and it was suddenly extremely important to know what this horse was named before he climbed onto it. *That's Jiminty. Other one's Peppermint.* Really? *Really what?*

You've got Jiminty, Dewmint, Peppermint, and Widow Maker? *So?* Oh never mind. The others were staring at Andrew, and he tried once more to grin. It still didn't work. "Sorry 'bout that. Just needed a minute. Um…we can go now?"

Charlie nodded and stood, quickly mounting his horse, and before Andrew knew it they were all mounted and waiting for him. He stared at Jiminty. It was so tall. There was no way he'd ever be able to mount it. *It ain't hard boy. You just put one foot in the stirrup, grab the saddle horn, and pull yourself up.* That didn't sound hard, but he wasn't going to do it with the others watching him.

Chapter Three

"You go ahead," Andrew said. "I gotta stretch my leg. I'll catch up."

Doyle's eyebrows shot up. "Stretch your leg?" he asked in disbelief.

"Yep, um, that cramp's a nasty bugger."

Doyle's eyes narrowed, and he started to open his mouth, but Charlie started riding, so Doyle just cast Andrew one last glare before following Charlie away from the sunset.

Andrew stared at the humongous horse. Is it nice? *What?* The horse? Pecos snorted. *You're a city slicker through and through, ain't ya?* But does it bite? *No she don't bite! Get your butt in the saddle, boy!*

Andrew wished he were anywhere but here, having any dream but this one. If it was a dream, which he was beginning to doubt. Which went against all logic as far as he was concerned, but still there was just something about it. He approached the horse cautiously.

"Jiminty, pretty Jiminty; you're a pretty horse aren't you?" *What the hell you doin'?* Talking to her. *That ain't talkin'; don't know what that is.* Andrew rolled his eyes. That was the way his mom always talked to dogs, and even if they were super nasty, they always calmed down and drooled all over her. Couldn't hurt to try it on the horse.

He reached out a shaking hand to stroke Jiminty's nose. "What a nice girl you are." Pecos started growling. "I'm just gonna, um...get on you now, okay?" Andrew looked at the things Pecos had called stirrups; they were really far off the ground. He tried to reach one with his foot, but he couldn't quite. He jumped for it, but didn't make it. Pecos was muttering, but Andrew ignored him.

There was a rock several feet away Andrew thought he could use as a stepping stone, but he didn't know how to get the horses to move over there. "Would you walk over there, please?" he asked, pointing. Jiminty twitched her tail, and Pecos called him a city slicker, thick-headed idiot. *Put your back into it! You're in my body; you can do everythin' I can do. Been mountin' horses since I was yea tall!* Andrew didn't know how much yea was, but he figured it was pretty short.

If he didn't get on this horse he was going to be stuck out here in the middle of...nowhere. He didn't see any towns or houses or roads, and there were no visible signs of human life. I shouldn't have told them to go ahead, he thought with a whisper of panic. He was lost; because if they got ahead of him, he didn't know where he was or where they were going.

Andrew grabbed the saddle horn and pulled, trying to drag himself into the saddle, but he barely moved. *That all you got, boy?* Andrew's cheeks heated. It's not my fault you weigh a ton! He felt like his arms were going to pull out of the sockets. He took a deep breath and jerked himself as hard as he could. He moved half a foot off the ground.

"Crap," he hissed, totally disgusted. "I can do this!" He grabbed the horn, stretched his leg as far as he could, barely hooked the toe of his boot into the stirrup, and pulled with all his might. Suddenly he was flying through the air and over the saddle. He landed face first on the other side of Jiminty with an awful thud.

Apparently Pecos was really, really strong. Andrew groaned, trying not to move. Everything hurt, and he was so tired of hurting. Maybe he should just pack it in, curl up under a tree, and wait to wake up. That would probably be the best plan. Why was he trying to be Pecos anyway? He didn't need to be Pecos. Sure it might have been fun to ride around and shoot things, but it wasn't worth it. Nothing was worth this.

Get your butt in the saddle! Now! I don't got time for this! Pecos, I'm not you. I'm not good at this. I don't know how to do any of this. I play baseball and fish. That's all I know how to do. Can't you push me out so I can go home? Pecos snorted. *You think I've just been sittin' here idle like waitin' for you to leave?* Um…yeah? *NO! I've been pushin' and kickin' and tearin', but you won't budge!* Oh.

So, you'll get up, and you'll get on the damn horse! NOW! Andrew sighed and pushed himself to his feet. He didn't know why he was doing this, why he was trying to be Pecos, but apparently he was. He grabbed the saddle, hooked his foot, and pulled. He pulled and pulled and pulled, and finally he did it! He was in the saddle! He was on the horse!

"I did it!" he exclaimed. *Yep, sure did. Just one teeny problem, boy.* What? *You're facin' the wrong way,* Pecos snarled.

Andrew looked down. Sure enough; Jiminty's tail was swishing the air in front of him. Well…damn. *Disgrace, embarrassment…* Pecos went on and on. Andrew sighed and tried to move his tired legs around, but ended up on the ground once more. His tailbone hurt. His face hurt. Everything hurt.

This was a bad day. A bad day in a long, long line of bad days, starting sometime last summer, worsening bit by bit when his dad didn't come home for his birthday or anything else, and absolutely tanking when he fell out of that stupid tree on the first day of summer vacation, breaking his leg in three places. In fact, if he was ordering bad days in his mind, this would be number three. Right behind his birthday and the day he broke his leg.

Andrew shoved his growing fear to the back of his mind and stared at the saddle. What did I do wrong? No wonder, he thought, laughing softly. I started with the wrong foot. He lifted his left foot, shoved it into the stirrup, grabbed the saddle horn, and pulled hard, landing in the saddle with a solid plop.

"I did it! Take that, Pecos! Not so city slicker now, am I?" *Nope; you're a real paragon of horsemanship.* Andrew rolled his eyes. No need to be a jerk. *This…this ain't good.* I'm sorry, Andrew thought, really meaning it. He was sorry, sorry he was here, sorry he couldn't do what Pecos wanted him to do, sorry he couldn't wake up.

Now what? *Better catch up.* But how? *Heels, boy, heels!* Oh, right. Andrew tapped his heels into Jiminty's side, and she started forward. How do I turn? *Reins; just pull the way you wanna go.* Pecos's voice was soft and frustrated. Andrew sighed, wishing once again he had ended up in a baseball dream, where he actually knew what he was doing.

He looked all around, but he couldn't see them. They had left him behind. He hadn't even seen which way they'd gone. He was lost! Lost and alone. *Quit your whinin'. Head east.*

Andrew pulled the reins to the right, and Jiminty turned away from the last bit of sun. He tapped his heels, and she went faster. He kept tapping until she was running. He held on with both hands, legs clutched. *Relax!* I can't! Andrew stared around anxiously. The sun was almost gone, and soon it would be dark. Are we gonna stop soon? *You can't have to pee again already!*

Heat flooded Andrew's face. No! It's just…it's almost dark. *So?* We can't ride in the dark. *Why not?* 'Cause it's DARK! Pecos sighed deeply. *This ain't gonna work.* What? *This! You!* I'm sorry. Andrew didn't know what else to say. Logically this was a dream. It wasn't real. What happened here didn't matter. But Pecos believed it was real, and he was upset. There was something Pecos needed to do, and Andrew was in his way.

He just wasn't cut out for this. The only thing he was good at was baseball. He couldn't do anything else. He was a lousy student, a lousy reader, a lousy tree climber; there really wasn't anything he was good at besides baseball. Why would this be any different?

You're gonna have to tell 'em. Who? *The others. You gotta tell 'em you're here.* "WHAT! Are you outta your mind?!" Jiminty jumped beneath him, and Andrew tried to loosen his legs. It was almost completely dark, and he couldn't see a thing. He couldn't see Charlie, he couldn't see the ground. He could see Jiminty's head and that was it. His stomach lurched. He hated the dark, and he'd never been in dark as dark as this.

Whistle. What? *Whistle; they'll come back around.* Andrew didn't want them to come back around, but he also didn't want to be all alone in the dark, so he whistled. It sounded loud and clear, piercing the dry air.

Now what? *Wait.* Jiminty was still racing into the dark. How do I stop? *Damn city slicker! Pull back on the reins...gently!* Andrew pulled on the reins, and Jiminty leaped to a halt. Andrew stayed perfectly still. He'd never been in such darkness in all his life. It was the total absence of light, and it was stifling. He couldn't breathe; he couldn't breathe.

Relax. Pecos's calm voice broke through his panic, and Andrew forced air into his lungs. So whadda you want me to say anyway? Andrew asked, trying to distract himself from the surrounding darkness. *Just tell 'em what it is.* And then what? *Well, I expect it'll go one of two ways.* Yeah? *Either they'll kill you or they'll help you.* WHAT?! Kill me?! Is that really on the table, I mean, I'm YOU! You're me! Suddenly the darkness didn't seem so bad.

Pecos chuckled, but he never answered, and it was too late anyway because the others had just ridden out of the darkness and were now surrounding Andrew. He could just barely see them through the gloom, and they looked...scary.

"What the hell's goin' on?" Doyle snapped.

"Nothing...I mean...um..."

"You alright?" the mustached man asked softly. For some reason Andrew couldn't remember his name.

"Um...yeah...I just..." I can't do this! You're right; they'll kill me! I can see it in their eyes. *You gotta, boy. Ain't gonna survive if you don't.* "It's super dark. Could we like make a fire or something?" Andrew pleaded.

"You wanna make camp?" Doyle asked incredulously.

Suddenly Andrew was very tired, so tired that sleeping on the ground beside three scary dudes didn't seem that bad. And that's when he knew. It wasn't a dream. It couldn't be a dream. Who ever heard of being sleepy in a dream? If he was already asleep, why would he be sleepy?

He stared out at the emptiness of everything. He heard the absolute quietness; or maybe it wasn't quiet, not really, just absent of all the sounds he was used to, cars, planes, air conditioners, music. He glanced up at the sky and gasped. He'd never seen the stars so bright, so brilliant, so beautiful. And there were so many!

His head swirled, and he felt sick. He needed his feet on the ground. He needed to touch the earth. He slipped off Jiminty, stumbling, but managed to catch himself, and then he vomited all over Pecos's boots.

Damn city slicker! You're cleanin' those, and you're cleanin' 'em good! And now Andrew was sure, without any doubt. He wasn't dreaming. How he wished he was! It didn't make any sense; it wasn't logical; it defied explanation. But Grandpa Lester had once said "if you've eliminated all the possible solutions, that which is impossible, becomes possible."

Andrew wiped his mouth with the back of his hand and straightened, freezing when he saw Doyle's gun trained directly at his head.

"Who the hell're you?" Doyle snarled. "'Cause you sure as hell ain't Pecos."

Andrew laughed softly, completely aware that if Doyle pulled the trigger he was dead. Not pretend dead, not wake-up-gasping dead, but dead. Really and truly dead. He held up his hands. "Can you make a fire?" Andrew asked. "I can't see."

"Make the fire, Doyle," the mustached man drawled. "I'll keep an eye on him." Andrew could barely see the outline of a gun barrel resting on the mustached man's saddle ridge.

Charlie hopped from his horse, took Jiminty's reins, and led the horses away. Doyle growled audibly, but holstered his gun and dismounted, following Charlie.

Andrew stood completely still, wishing he had some water to wash the vomit taste from his mouth. "I forgot your name," he said awkwardly. "There's Charlie and Doyle and you are?"

"Joe."

"That's right. Thanks."

Idiot boy. If you get us killed I'll haunt you for... What? The rest of my life? I'll be dead too, duh! *Boy...* Andrew tried to ignore Pecos and focus on what he knew. He knew he was in Pecos's body, so where was his body? Pecos Bill was just a legend, so where was he? In a book? Or was Pecos Bill just a legend? Sometimes legends were based on real people. Was he in the past somewhere? But how had he gotten here? He shook his head. He couldn't believe he was even thinking like this. He must be insane.

An orange glow suddenly filled the night, and Andrew sighed in relief. He wasn't scared of the dark; he really wasn't. But there was a big difference between this dark and the dark he knew.

"Come on," Joe said, motioning towards the fire. Andrew stepped forward and tripped, nearly falling over his feet. "You might want to clean off your boots," Joe drawled lazily.

"How?" Andrew asked, staring in dismay at Pecos's vomit covered boots. Pecos went off on another rant, something about city slickers who didn't even know how to clean up messes, and Andrew sighed. Forget third place. This day, whatever day it was, was number one. Of all his bad days, this was the worst.

Chapter Four

After Andrew had rubbed the vomit off Pecos's boots with a handful of dirt and dried grass, he walked slowly to the fire and sat across from the others, the fire sparking between them, casting light on their hard faces. Doyle held a cup of steaming liquid in one hand and his gun in the other, barrel trained steadily at Andrew.

"You a spirit?" Charlie asked.

"A spirit? Like a ghost?" Charlie nodded, and Andrew paled. He hadn't thought of that. What if he was already dead? What if he had died and his spirit had wandered all over the place until it somehow settled in Pecos's body? "I don't know," he mumbled. "The last thing I remember was sitting in bed reading some stupid story about Pecos Bill."

"Stupid story?" Joe asked.

"He's not real!" Andrew exclaimed, truly wanting to believe it. "None of you are real..." Only he didn't believe it; it was real; he knew it was real; he just didn't know how. *You still too much a fool to believe what you can see and feel?* Andrew didn't answer. He couldn't talk to Pecos and them at the same time.

"Ain't real?" Doyle growled. "How 'bout I shoot you, and we see how real I am?"

"I'd really rather you didn't," Andrew whispered, knowing the bullet would hurt, knowing he would bleed.

"So who are you?" Joe asked.

"Andrew Rufus."

"Ain't never heard of you," Doyle snapped.

Andrew rolled his eyes. "Of course you haven't. I'm just a kid, and...what year is this anyway?"

"1867," Joe said.

Andrew had known he was in the past, but hearing it said out loud still shocked him a bit. How was it even possible? Time travel didn't exist. It just didn't. Did it? He was so confused.

"Is that before or after the Civil War?" he asked hesitantly, wishing he'd paid more attention in history class.

"After," Doyle snarled, face even darker than before.

"Oh. Well, um...I'm...like, not from this time." Andrew said carefully.

Charlie sat up straighter. "What time are you from?"

"Um...'bout a hundred and fifty years in the future. Give or take a few years."

They looked at him blankly for a moment, before Doyle snorted. "Give me one good reason why I shouldn't just shoot you and be done with it."

Pecos! Help! *You seem to be doin' real good on your own.* No; I'm not. Please help. Pecos sighed. *I'd start by tellin' 'em I'm still here.* Of course! Andrew felt stupid he hadn't thought of that.

"Pecos is still in here!" he exclaimed.

"What do you mean?" Joe asked.

"Inside my head. He keeps yelling at me and calling me names and stuff."

"Sounds like Pecos," Joe said with a slight grin.

Charlie leaned forward, eyes narrowed. "Prove it," he said softly.

"Prove it?!" Andrew exclaimed. "How?"

"Just prove it."

Pecos! *What?* Prove it! Do you wanna die? Pecos muttered something, then he said irritably, *Ask 'em if they 'member that time one of my brothers snuck into the hen house and ate all the eggs and one of the hens. Enrica wouldn't speak to me for a week.* That didn't make any sense to Andrew, but he shrugged and said, "Pecos says to ask you if you remember the time one of his brothers snuck into the hen house and ate all the eggs and one of the hens. He says Enrica wouldn't talk to him for a week."

"I don't see how anyone else'd know that," Charlie said thoughtfully. "You some kinda witch?"

"What?! No! I'm a just boy. I'm only thirteen. I don't know how I got here or how to get out. I don't know anything," Andrew insisted.

"Thirteen," Doyle snorted. "Practically a man."

Andrew shook his head. "Not where I'm from. I mean I can only just now stay home alone."

"That don't make no sense," Doyle snapped.

"Just the way it is," Andrew said with a shrug. *Figures I'd get stuck with a city slicker boy who don't even know how to clean his own boots.* Andrew wanted to argue, but honestly, he didn't. His mom took care of everything. The most Andrew could do was open the refrigerator door and make a piece of toast. *Chuck is right;* he thought ruefully. *I am a momma's boy.*

"I can't believe I didn't realize right away," Joe was saying. "He doesn't talk at all like Pecos, and look at the way he's sitting. If only Pecos could see him."

How you sittin'?! Huh? Same way I always sit. *Well quit it!* Andrew sighed. He didn't know how to sit any other way especially with Pecos's long legs, but he looked across the fire at Doyle and tried to splay his legs out like Doyle's were.

Charlie shrugged. "Saw it right off."

"Whadda you mean?" Doyle growled.

"Eye color changed."

"What?!" Doyle jumped to his feet and stalked to Andrew, who sat frozen solid, staring wide-eyed as Doyle's gun came closer and closer. Doyle peered into Andrew's face before pulling back and whispering, "Well I'll be damned."

"What color are Pecos's eyes?" Andrew asked shakily, wishing Doyle would put the gun away.

"Blue as a robin's egg," Joe said, looking into Andrew's face as well. "Sure enough. Can't believe I missed that."

"Damned bad timing," Doyle muttered.

"Why's that?" Andrew asked. "Pecos keeps talking about a snake, but surely you guys can handle it?"

Joe laughed merrily, and Charlie shook his head. "Something black whispered in the father of all snakes' ear, and he has risen from his rest angry and vengeful."

Charlie shrugged before adding, "At least that's what Grandmother said."

"The father of all snakes? For real?"

The three of them nodded, and Doyle poured himself more steaming black liquid. "What is that?" Andrew asked.

"Coffee." Doyle paused for a moment, before holstering his gun, pouring another cup, and offering it to Andrew.

"Um...I'm not allowed to drink coffee," Andrew said awkwardly.

"What?" Joe and Doyle asked together.

"Mom says it'll stunt my growth."

Joe started laughing again. "Won't stunt nothin'," Doyle growled. "'Sides you in Pecos's body now. You best have some." Andrew took the cup with trembling hands. He was fairly certain they weren't going to kill him now; he wasn't sure why, and he wasn't going to ask. But he figured he'd better drink the coffee if he wanted to keep it that way.

He took a cautious sip. It burned like hell and slid down his throat leaving a thick coating that felt like tar. "You sure that's coffee?" he gasped.

Doyle grinned widely, reminding Andrew of a wolf he'd once seen in a zoo. "My specialty."

Good for you, boy. Andrew cringed, taking a second, smaller sip. At least his mouth didn't taste like puke anymore. "Where are we?" Andrew asked.

"Somewhere between Texas and New Mexico Territory," Joe responded.

"Huh. So what now?"

"What's Pecos say?" Joe replied.

Pecos? *Huh?* Whadda we do now? Pecos didn't get a chance to respond before the air around the fire suddenly shifted, and a tall man with long, shimmery grey hair and a grey cloak appeared out of nothingness. Andrew stared, mouth hanging. "Where did...what?" *Damn shaman,* Pecos growled.

The man looked around the fire, raised one brow, and said, "Where is...oh...never mind, I see now." Then he started laughing. "You would think after all this time I would get it right," he chuckled softly.

"Get what right?" Andrew asked, still reeling from shock.

"Oh, nothing. Just a little something I was working on." He stared at Andrew intently for a moment. "Interesting. Who's who? Ah, I see now. The boy is in charge."

Andrew's heart jumped. "What? How did...who are you?!"

"Pecos calls me the Grey Shaman," he said with a wink. "I am not a shaman, but he doesn't seem to grasp that."

Do magic don't you? Meddle with stuff don't you? My book that's a shaman. Or a witch.

"I do prefer shaman to witch. Exudes mystery."

Andrew gasped. "You heard him? How did you hear him?"

"Shaman, remember?"

Andrew couldn't keep up. First he'd time traveled and body snatched and now magic truly existed because here was someone who could do it, magic.

And Andrew knew he could because he'd popped in out of nothing; and frankly, no one else seemed the least bit surprised.

"Anyway," the Grey Shaman said. "I was just passing by. Wanted to say good day."

Pecos snorted. *What's in it for you?*

"Pecos, you wound me. I see Doyle made the coffee. I'll stop by again when Charlie's made it." And just like that he was gone.

Andrew stared at the place he'd been. "Who...? What...? I mean, how?"

"Cat's got the boy's tongue," Joe said laughingly.

"Might as well rest for the night," Charlie said before anyone else could speak. "Figure out what we're gonna do in the mornin'. The boy ain't gonna be able to keep up at night. He's a terrible rider."

"Hey!" Andrew snapped. He wasn't terrible; he'd just never done it; and as a rule, he only did things he was good at and avoided things he wasn't good at. But he was pretty sure that wasn't going to be an option here. Even if he was a terrible rider, it was either ride or get left behind.

He should have asked the Grey Shaman guy if he knew how he'd gotten here. Or, even better, if he knew how to send him back. Andrew didn't want to sleep here. He didn't want to sleep because if he slept here and woke up here, he'd have no choice but to believe it was real. He already knew it was real, but sleeping would make it too real. So real he wouldn't be able to think it wasn't. *You ain't makin' sense, boy.*

"I would've liked to have seen Pecos's face when the boy fell off his horse," Joe said chuckling.

"Worst horseman ever," Doyle added with a grunt.

"Can you just imagine," Joe went on. "Pecos riding around inside while the boy's falling on his face and looking like a fool?" Joe started laughing so hard he couldn't talk.

Andrew rolled his eyes. He was sitting right here. And his name was Andrew, not BOY. He sighed as Doyle and Charlie started laughing too. *It was a bit funny.* Not you too. *You're truly awful. Lousiest rider I've ever seen.* Then to make everything worse, Pecos started laughing too.

Andrew closed his eyes and waited for it to end. When the laughing finally died down, he kept his eyes closed, wondering what would happen next. An odd musical sound floated into the crisp night air, and Andrew opened his eyes again. Joe was playing a harmonica, and the music was strange to Andrew but absolutely beautiful. Andrew felt it pull at him, and he knew he'd never heard anything as simply perfect.

Charlie tossed Andrew a saddle blanket and said softly, "Go to sleep, boy. We'll figure out what to do in the mornin'."

Andrew suddenly wished they'd kept riding. He'd never slept away from his mom in his life, and he missed her. He shook his head ruefully. He couldn't believe he'd climbed that damn tree trying to prove Chuck wrong. If anything he'd proved him right.

He tried to imagine his mom tucking him in and kissing his head, ruffling his hair and telling him goodnight. He imagined the bright, glow-in-the-dark stars she had painted on his ceiling. Her story about the boy who befriended the dark ran through his head. He wished he was that brave, as brave as the little boy who'd found there was nothing to fear. But he was in the dark now, and he was very much afraid.

He closed his eyes, pushing thoughts of his mom away, and listened to Joe's music. The eerie melody soothed him, calming him; and for a moment he stopped thinking and just felt. Felt the crisp, clean air, the hard ground, the warmth of the fire, and then he gave in to the exhaustion trying to pull him under and drifted off to sleep.

Andrew dreamed, and it was shockingly vivid. So vivid he wondered for a second if it wasn't a dream, but he didn't have a body. He was just watching, floating around in the dark. He saw dark paths underground, deep caves, and damp caverns. He heard a sinister whispering voice. A voice mixing truth with lies; a voice full of hate. When the voice spoke, it woke something old, something ancient; woke it and whispered lies in its ear. The ancient being grew angry, so angry the earth shook. And when the being reared its head and roared to the sky, the earth burst out all around it, exploding into the air; and the ancient one slithered out into the bright light of day.

Andrew woke gasping for air and fumbling for his light switch. But his light switch wasn't there. It wasn't there because he was lying on the ground in the middle of nowhere, and everything was still dark except for the soft, orange blaze of the fire. He steadied his breath, staring across the barely lit fire, jumping as his eyes met Doyle's cold, hard gaze and everything came flooding back. He had wanted to believe it was a dream; he had wanted to believe it was some drug-induced trip, but he knew, he knew it wasn't. He didn't know how he knew. He just knew.

'Bout time you woke up, Pecos grumbled. *Get movin'.* Where? *Gotta stop a snake, boy; don't you listen?* And then Andrew remembered his dream. No way! he gasped. Is "father of all snakes" code for unbelievably enormous snake? *Haven't seen 'im, but he's probably purty big.* No, no, and NO! I'm not going! No way; no how!

Boy... No way! You haven't seen it, but I have, and it's huge, like as long as a train huge, as wide as an interstate huge! *Boy*... No, no, no! *Listen*... NO, YOU LISTEN!!! I may be in your body, but I can't do the things you say you can do. For crap's sake, I can't even ride a horse! I can't fight for you! I'm not a hero or a legend or even a really strong guy. I'm me, Andrew Rufus. I fall out of trees. That's what I do.

Listen boy! Pecos snapped. *You're in my body, and while you may not know what to do, my body damn well does! All you gotta do is stop gettin' in the way.* I don't know how to do that! *Learn! I ain't never been sore, ever! I ain't never fallen off a horse. I ain't never puked my guts out. My body don't do those things. You gotta stop thinkin' like YOU and start thinkin' like ME!* That doesn't make any sense! *Sure it does!* Pecos snapped. Andrew wrapped his hands around his head.

He couldn't' believe he was arguing with a voice INSIDE his head. Only it wasn't his head, was it?

Anyway, you don't got no choice. You mount; you ride; you fight. Or what? *Or... I'll yell and yell and yell and yell until you can't stand it no more!* This is life and death; I could die! Literally die! And you think I'm gonna go die 'cause you're gonna yell at me? *People're dyin'! We can stop it.* No, YOU can. I can't. *Boy...* I'm not going!

Suddenly a hot cup was in Andrew's hands, the steam rising and warming his cheeks. He frowned and looked up. Joe grinned and handed Andrew a plate of food. If it could be called that. "What's this?" Andrew asked.

"Rabbit and biscuits."

"Those are biscuits?" Andrew asked, poking at the hard, semi-black lumps on his plate.

"Doyle makes them."

Andrew paled. He certainly wasn't going to complain about something Doyle had made. "Yum," he said softly, missing his mom's breakfasts. She loved to cook, and her biscuits looked nothing like these. She'd cringe if she saw him eating this, but his stomach was growling fiercely, so he started eating.

Joe sat beside him, eating neatly, with impossible manners for someone eating without a table or a fork. "How you doing this morning?" he asked amiably.

"I'm sore," Andrew grunted. "And Pecos wants me to fight some gigantic snake for him. It's laughable."

"Why's that?"

"Have you seen me? It took me seven tries to get on a stupid horse."

"That is a lot, but have you ever mounted a horse before?"

"No, but still."

The biscuits were so hard and dry, Andrew had to drink the coffee just to wash them down. It rushed burning down his throat, warming him from the inside out. He shrugged; maybe coffee wasn't all that bad.

"All you need is some training," Joe said.

"Are you out of your mind?! Why can't you guys do it anyway?"

"Well, Pecos really just brought us along for the company. He doesn't actually need our help, and we're not…we're not Pecos, you see?"

"No, I don't see. What's so special about Pecos?"

"Everything," Joe said with a grin.

Andrew rolled his eyes, but before he could say anything, Joe continued talking lazily. "I understand you don't want to be Pecos, but we've got to ride over there and see what's what, and you may as well come with us."

"No way! That snake is a monster," Andrew said firmly.

"You've seen him?" Joe asked in surprise.

"Well, no, but um…" Andrew took a drink of coffee, but it didn't help him think of an answer. "Well, I had a dream," he finally mumbled.

"Much can be learned from dreams," Charlie said from across the fire.

"In any case, you'd better come," Joe said, tone relaxed. "You don't have to fight or do anything you don't want to." Pecos started ranting and raving, but Andrew ignored him. He liked what Joe was saying better.

"But," Joe added, "We can't rightly leave you here. All alone."

Andrew's eyes grew wide. He hadn't thought about them leaving him. He'd starve; he'd die of thirst; he'd get eaten by hungry pumas. *You idiot! As if a cougar would dare!*

"Okay," Andrew said quickly. "I'll come with you. But I'm not doing anything."

"Well," Joe said slowly. "You might as well do some training on the way, get comfortable in Pecos's skin, don't you think?"

Andrew didn't think. He didn't want to be comfortable in Pecos's skin. He wanted to go home. He wanted to taste his mom's pancakes with maple syrup. He wanted to watch the neon stars glow on his ceiling. But he knew he wasn't going to. He was stuck here. Was he going to be here forever? Was this his life now? Would he never see his own face and hands again? *You best hope that ain't the case,* Pecos growled.

Chapter Five

Andrew sat in silence for a moment, wondering what he was going to do, but his thoughts were broken when the entire plain was suddenly bathed in brilliant light. Joe slipped a watch out of his vest pocket. Flipping the cover open he looked at the time, then glanced at the blazing sun that was just slipping over the horizon. "Right on time," he murmured with a grin, snapping the lid closed again. The sun glinted off the gold casing as Joe slipped the watch back into his pocket.

"Let's mount up," Charlie said.

Andrew didn't know how to do that. He had never felt so helpless in his entire life. Joe, Charlie, and Doyle weren't going to do things for him like his mom did; they were going to make him do it. Because not only would he almost be a man if he were here in his own body, but he was also in a literal man's body. They might hand him a plate of food, but that was it; he was going to have to learn how to do everything else.

He followed them to the horses, trying to remember which three were Pecos's. They all looked the same to him, but he figured the three tallest had to be Pecos's. "Are those Pecos's?" he asked pointing.

Charlie nodded. "Dewmint's got the star, Peppermint's the buckskin, Jiminty's the grey one." Andrew didn't know what a buckskin was but guessed by process of elimination it was the brown one.

He limped as he stepped forward. His feet, legs, and back hurt with every step he took, so he stopped and tried to touch his toes. *BOY!* Get over it; I'm stiff. *Wouldn't be stiff if you could ride worth a damn.* Whatever. Andrew stretched his arms up and leaned to the side.

"What you doin'?" Charlie asked, staring at him.

"Stretching."

"Huh; Pecos alright with that?"

Andrew snorted. "No, but I'm the one who's sore so he's just gonna have to deal with it." He bent his knee and pulled his foot towards his back. His muscles screamed. *Boy, if you keep doin' this I'm gonna beat you up one side and down the other.* Really? How? Pecos just growled.

"Alright," Andrew said, dropping his leg. "Which one am I riding?"

"Start with Peppermint."

"I need the saddle, right?"

Doyle snorted from where his horse was already saddled and ready to go. "We should just leave 'im here. Let the buzzards have 'im."

Andrew's heart jumped. He may not want to ride a horse, he may not want to know how to saddle a horse, but he'd better learn and he'd better learn quickly, because if he didn't, Doyle might leave him here, and he'd be stuck with Pecos alone. It was possible it would be better to die fighting a gigantic snake than to die in the wilderness with Pecos yelling at him.

Andrew found his saddle and stared at it. There were so many parts, but he recognized the horn from yesterday, so he knew that part went towards the horse's head. So, first things first, he thought, put the saddle on. *Saddle blanket!* Oh, right. Andrew grabbed the saddle blanket and approached the brown horse carefully.

"Pretty horsey. I like your hair. It's um…long." *Idiot boy. It's a mane.* Andrew kept talking nonsense until he had the saddle blanket on Peppermint. Peppermint gave him a long look, but otherwise stayed still.

Then Andrew bent to lift the saddle. Wow! This is heavy! *Ain't heavy; in fact that's a lightweight saddle.* Andrew rolled his eyes. Everything they did was big. They rode big horses, had big saddles, wore big hats. He wondered if there was some cowboy rulebook somewhere that said everything had to be such and such size. He struggled to lift the saddle from the ground, then stared at Peppermint's wide back. There was no way he'd ever be able to get it up there.

Shame…disgrace…city slicker…torment… Pecos went on and on. Andrew wondered if this was the first time in Pecos's life things hadn't gone his way. *Never gonna let me forget this.* Andrew heaved the saddle, but didn't get it high enough.

"Need help?" Joe asked somewhat doubtfully.

"I can do it," Andrew muttered. He didn't want to be a momma's boy; he didn't want to be weak. He could do this; he just had to figure out how. *Got all the strength you need in my arms, boy. Just use it!* Andrew frowned. He knew Pecos was strong. He'd felt it when he'd flown over Jiminty. But as Andrew in Pecos, Andrew wasn't any stronger than Andrew. He bit his lip and tried to summon strength into his arms.

He stepped closer and tried to imagine he was Pecos and he was doing something he did every day, lifting a saddle onto a horse. He swung, and the saddle whipped through the air, barely, just barely, clearing Peppermint's back. It landed all willy-nilly, stirrups all over the place, but Andrew grinned in triumph. He'd done it! He'd gotten the saddle on the horse.

It took him a while to get everything straightened out. Instead of complaining, Pecos gave him clear instructions on which straps to buckle first and what went where. By the time Andrew was done, the sun was much higher in the sky, and Doyle was brimming with irritation.

Now all Andrew had to do was mount. He remembered to put his left foot in first, and then he pulled hard and swung himself into the saddle. He landed with a plop, groaning as pain shot through his body.

"'Bout time!" Doyle snapped.

"Stay by me," Charlie told Andrew, turning his horse towards the sun and riding out of their camp.

Andrew tapped Peppermint softly with his heels, using the reins to guide her after Charlie. Did you see that, Pecos? I did it! *Sure; only took you an hour.* Andrew sighed. He'd done it, hadn't he? An hour probably wasn't bad for his first time. Never mind

Pecos could probably do it in under a minute. He wasn't Pecos. He just wished Pecos could get that through his thick skull.

Charlie didn't speak for a while, and Andrew's mind wandered. He wondered what his mom was doing. He wondered if it had been a day there or a year or just a minute. He wondered if he was still alive. He hoped he was. He couldn't bear the thought of her crying over his dead body. He was her baby, her only child; it would just be too cruel.

"You gotta be one with your horse," Charlie said suddenly.

"What?"

"One with your horse."

"How?"

"Move with the rhythm. Each horse's got its own rhythm. Close your eyes and find it."

Andrew's hands tightened on the reins. "Close my eyes? Are you crazy? What if I run into something?"

Charlie chuckled softly. "Peppermint's doin' most of the work, not you."

Andrew supposed that made sense. He hadn't really guided Dewmint yesterday. She'd just followed the others. "Fine," he grumbled. He hated to do it, but he closed his eyes. He gasped, knowing he was going to fall, but he didn't.

"Relax your back; relax your legs," Charlie said.

Andrew breathed deeply, trying to imagine he was up at bat, about to swing. He relaxed his hold on the reins, relaxed his legs, relaxed his whole body. He couldn't hit the ball if he was clenched up.

"Better. Feel the rhythm?"

Andrew didn't, but then he noticed there was a steady bounce every time Peppermint took a step. He tried to relax so his body could move with hers, and he started breathing in time with the bounce. "A little faster now," Charlie said.

Andrew almost opened his eyes, but if he was going to survive he needed to learn to trust Charlie and Peppermint, so he tapped his heels softly and felt Peppermint's pace increase. "Feel the change in her rhythm?" Charlie asked.

Andrew could, but he couldn't seem to move with Peppermint the same as he'd been able to when she was walking. "Go a bit faster," Charlie urged. Andrew didn't want to go any faster, but he tapped his heels again, and Peppermint sped up, her rhythm changing again. Andrew gasped and gripped the reins tighter.

Relax, boy. You can do this. Well, my body can do it anyway. Andrew actually laughed, breathing out and forcing himself to relax once more. *Horse is the most important part of being a cowboy.* Really? I would have thought it was the cows. COWboy. *Shows what you know.*

"Faster," Charlie said.

Andrew groaned, but tapped his heels. This time Peppermint moved so fast, Andrew felt sure he'd fly off onto the ground, breaking all his bones, but he didn't. In fact, even though Peppermint was virtually flying, her rhythm was so smooth, it was easy for Andrew to relax.

How long he rode like that, eyes closed, Peppermint gliding beneath him, he didn't know. But suddenly he was falling. His eyes snapped open just as a rope settled around him, pulling him upright in the saddle again.

"What happened?" he gasped. *Fell asleep you idiot!*

"Must've drifted off," Charlie said grinning.

Andrew shook the sleep from his head and pushed the rope over his shoulders. Joe rolled the rope back in, grin wide under his mustache. Doyle was shaking his head disgustedly. "Thanks, Joe," Andrew muttered, feeling stupid.

"Sure thing."

"So how long until we get there?"

"Hour; less," Charlie said.

"WHAT?!" Andrew needed longer than that. He wasn't ready. He could barely ride. But through his panic he remembered he didn't have to do anything. He was just going to watch. *Just gonna watch? You insane? I don't watch. I do.* But I don't. So…whatever. Pecos went off on a rant that had Andrew's ears stinging, but what could he do? He was just a kid. He didn't know anything about guns or ropes or knives. He was useless here. *Damn right you are!*

"How do you know we're so close?" Andrew asked.

"Just do."

Andrew rolled his eyes. That wasn't an answer. Pecos stopped ranting long enough to snap, *If Charlie says we're close, we're close.* Then he started yelling again about lily-livered, city boys.

No one spoke as they continued to ride, and Andrew tried to ignore Pecos and focus on relaxing into the rhythm. He wasn't going to fight the father of all snakes. It didn't matter what Pecos said or yelled or accused. But he did have to ride a horse if he didn't want to get left all alone in the desert or plains or wilderness, whatever it was.

It wasn't long before Andrew could hear it. He didn't know what he was hearing, but he knew it was the snake, and he wished he could ride the other way. Can you die? he asked Pecos suddenly. *What?* Can you die? Are you immortal? *What? No, I mean, yes.* Yes, you can die? *Yes! Just a man.*

Andrew's heart thudded a little harder as Charlie pushed his horse into a run, and Andrew and the others followed after him. They crested a hill, and Andrew gasped, wishing he were anywhere but here. A small town lay nestled in the valley beneath them, road running in one side and out the other. And just inside the town was a snake so enormous it took Andrew's breath away.

Its body was unbelievably long. The front part was inside the town, but Andrew couldn't see its tail because it was hidden between two hills outside the town. The snake's head was raised above the ground, just like a viper Andrew had once seen in a movie, and the part off the ground was easily a couple stories tall. The sun glinted off its green and orange scales like a mirror ball, making everything seem totally surreal. Andrew's dream hadn't done it justice. *Bit bigger than I expected.*

Charlie, Joe, and Doyle cut their spares loose and were flying down the hill, straight towards the town, and Peppermint was following them. Andrew pulled back frantically on his reins; Peppermint tossed her head, but slowed to a walk. *What're you doin'?* Nothing. *Get down there!* And do what? *Fight!* How Pecos? I've never touched a gun in my life! I've never been in a fight! I've never so much as punched a…anything! I'm not you!

Absolute horror filled Andrew as he watched the snake. It was beyond huge, and as it moved forward its body twisted, rolling over houses and buildings, crushing them beneath its incredible weight. The screams of the townsfolk nearly drowned out the cracking and snapping sounds of the boards, and they echoed off the hills and pounded Andrew's ears. He slapped his hands over them, trying to block it out.

Men were shooting the snake, but nothing seemed to hurt it; it just kept moving forward, crushing men and horses under its massive flesh. The woman and children were running the other way, running down the road out the other side of the town, but Andrew knew they could never outrun the snake. It was just too damn big.

BOY!!!! What?! *Get down there!* Andrew shook his head, fear choking him. He couldn't help them. He'd just die like they were, and he didn't want to die. He hadn't even lived yet. He hadn't pitched in a major league game. He hadn't seen the ocean. He hadn't ever told his mom how much he loved her.

Doyle, Joe, and Charlie had just reached the other men and joined the fight, and Andrew watched horrified as Charlie loosed arrow after arrow. Nothing slowed it down; nothing stopped it. The snake slithered forward, body ripping through boardwalks and structures, but Doyle, Joe, and Charlie moved backwards quickly, clearly better at fighting than the other men, many of whom didn't move fast enough and were caught under the snake's heavy body as it advanced.

The snake was halfway through the town now, leaving behind a trail of brokenness. Andrew couldn't just keep watching; he couldn't. The snake was slaughtering everyone, destroying everything. He swiped a tear from his eye. Maybe he couldn't do anything. Maybe he was just a boy, but he wasn't going to do nothing. He couldn't.

He fumbled with the leads for the spares. Finally they were loose, and he nudged Peppermint forward, terror making him sick. The snake's head swiveled left and right, jaws wide, fangs shining white in the sun. Suddenly its head snapped down, jaws closing around one of the men in front of him.

What would you do? he asked Pecos desperately. *If guns don't work, I'd beat it to the ground.* I can't do that. *GET OUT OF MY BODY, BOY!* Pecos yelled angrily. *Get out now!* Andrew closed his eyes and tried. He really, really tried. He imagined his room; he imagined his mom shaking him awake; he pinched his hand so hard he broke the skin. But his room didn't appear, and he stayed firmly in place.

I'm sorry. I'm so sorry. Andrew wanted to cry, but he forced the tears back and rode forward. At the edge of the town he turned away from the snake. *What you doin'? You runnin' away, you coward?* No, I'm not. I can't fight that thing! No one can! All you have is guns and knives. Doyle, Joe, and Charlie have those. If they can't kill it, neither can I. But maybe I can help the others. Andrew pushed Peppermint quickly down the road towards the women and children.

They were already flagging, fear strangling them, and he rode right behind them before reining Peppermint in. "This way!" he shouted, pointed towards the hills. He didn't know why, but he felt sure the snake was following the road. If they stayed on the road, they were dead.

The townspeople ignored him, so Andrew rode Peppermint in front of them. "Into the hills!" he shouted. "You can't outrun it!" They didn't listen; they just kept running, leaving the town behind them, but not leaving the road. Pecos! Whadda I do? *Nothin' to do.* Whadda you mean?! These people are gonna die! *Ain't listenin'.*

Andrew struggled to dismount, falling, but landing on his feet. He heard the crash of the buildings behind him, and when he glanced back, he saw the snake towering high above the town, high above the buildings and men. He could see its green glittering eyes, full of anger and hate; he could see globs of venom drop from its fangs and sizzle through the roofs.

He had to get these people off the road. He grabbed one of the women. "Listen to me! You have to head into the hills. It's the only way you can hide!" The woman pushed Andrew's hands away, eyes panicked, mouth open, screaming. She stumbled past him and kept running. Andrew grabbed a passing boy. "Into the hills!" he ordered. The boy shrieked, ripped his hand free, and ran after the others.

Andrew glanced back. The snake was at the edge of the town now, and only Doyle, Joe, and Charlie were left. They were the only ones fighting it; everyone else was dead. They couldn't win; they couldn't stop it; there was nothing they could do.

Mount up, boy, Pecos said, voice drawn. But…they'll die! *Nothin' you can do.* But… *MOUNT UP!* Andrew tried one last time. He shouted loudly, so loud it hurt even his own ears, "OFF THE ROAD! INTO THE HILLS!" But if anyone heard him, they ignored him and just kept running along the road.

Andrew choked on a sob and grabbed his saddle, pulling himself up. He rode towards the snake, mesmerized by its twisting green and orange scales. He rode until he was close enough that when it smashed through the last remaining building, debris flew past his face.

"COME ON!" Andrew screamed, turning Peppermint towards the hills and hoping the snake wouldn't pursue him. He didn't look back to see if the others followed. Somehow he knew they would. He rode and rode, passing the spares, assuming they would follow too, riding back over the hill, riding until he was sure when he stopped he wouldn't be able to see the snake, wouldn't see the people on the road die.

Chapter Six

Andrew sat on Peppermint, shaking, breath coming hard, searching behind him. Relief flooded him when he saw the others crest the hill, bringing the spares with them. He couldn't see or hear the snake any more. It hadn't followed them. It had followed the road, just like Andrew had thought it would. He tried not to think about all those people, all those dead people, and when the others pulled up beside him, he stared at the ground, scared to look at them, scared he would see disgust and hatred in their eyes.

"Well," Joe drawled. "This is not good."

"I'm sorry," Andrew stuttered. "I tried...I tried to get them to leave the road; I tried to get them to hide, but they wouldn't. They wouldn't listen to me."

He dismounted shakily and leaned his head against Peppermint, trying desperately not to vomit, not to see the crushed bodies or the terror in the fleeing boy's eyes, trying not to imagine what had happened next.

He flinched when a hand gripped his shoulder and squeezed tightly. "There wasn't anything you could do, boy," Joe said. "Only one who could've stopped that thing is Pecos."

Andrew whirled around, suddenly angry at them, at all of them. "That's bull!" he yelled. "That snake is humongous! It shouldn't even be called a snake.

Snakes are tiny, and you can step on them if you want to." Andrew was screaming, but he couldn't stop himself. It shouldn't exist. It shouldn't. It wasn't part of his world, and he simply couldn't wrap his head around it.

"It's a goliath serpent, a colossal monster!" he went on. "Bullets and arrows didn't even faze it! What could Pecos possibly have that a gun doesn't? WHAT?!"

"Everything," Joe said softly.

"Everything?! What does that even mean?!" Andrew's head was spinning, his throat was tight, and his stomach was rolling like mad. He just wanted to go home. He wanted snakes to be normal sized, he wanted Pecos Bill to be a stupid character in a lame book, and he wanted time travel to be a scientific impossibility.

"He's just a man!" Andrew yelled desperately. "He said he's just a man. He can DIE! Just like you and Charlie and Doyle. If you can't kill it why would he be able to?!"

"Pecos ain't just a man," Doyle snapped. "He's more...just more. When Pecos comes, trouble gets outta the way, and if it doesn't...well, it don't live to talk 'bout it."

"He once stopped a fifty-man shootout just by walking into the town," Joe said.

"When I was a boy he saved my people from a flood," Charlie added. "He dug a trench 'round the entire village right before the water hit. Never seen anyone do what he did."

Andrew laughed scornfully. "Those are just tall tales! Stories! Legends someone made up! That's not the man. The man is a man! No one can dig a trench big enough to stop a flood! That's ridiculous!"

"I know you don't have any reason to trust us yet," Joe said seriously. "But you'll just have to trust us on this. Pecos would tie that snake down in three minutes flat and give it such a good talking to it never came back."

Andrew frowned, struggling to understand what they were saying. If that was true, if Pecos was some kind of super-human being, which they honestly seemed to believe he was, then this was Andrew's fault. All those dead people, all those children, that town. It was his fault.

"So if it wasn't for me," he whispered, "those people wouldn't have died."

"Ain't precisely true," Charlie said.

"How do you figure?"

"You didn't put yourself in Pecos's body. Someone else did. So those deaths aren't on you; they're on whoever brought you here."

Andrew hadn't thought of that. For some reason he'd thought this was just some random, freak occurrence, but what if someone had brought him here on purpose? But why? Why would anyone want him? He was nobody. Andrew paled as a terrible thought occurred to him. What if someone's trying to kill you? *They'll be sorely disappointed.* Andrew wasn't sure about that. Pecos might be amazing, but Andrew wasn't.

"What're we gonna do?" Andrew asked. "That snake is just gonna keep on going down the road. Killing people. We've gotta stop him."

"Sure," Joe said. "But how? Pecos got any ideas?"

Pecos? Andrew asked. *I'm thinkin' on it. Tell Charlie I wanna see Grandma.* "Um…Charlie, Pecos wants to see Grandma?" Andrew hoped Charlie knew what that meant, because it didn't make any sense to him.

Charlie nodded. "Switch horses; then we ride."

Andrew was relieved that Joe and Charlie didn't seem disgusted by what he'd done or hadn't done. They believed Pecos could kill the snake, but they didn't expect Andrew to. Andrew snuck a look at Doyle, but he was staring back at the town, face motionless and hard. Andrew could tell he hadn't liked losing, riding off, leaving people behind to die. Andrew hadn't liked it either.

"Why wouldn't they listen to me?" Andrew whispered.

"Sometimes they just won't," Joe said. "Get Jiminty saddled."

Andrew nodded numbly, unbuckling and dragging the saddle off Peppermint and struggling to throw it over Jiminty's back. *Wipe Peppermint down,* Pecos said after Andrew had buckled all the buckles. How? *Use some grass.* Andrew ripped up a handful of grass and rubbed Peppermint down, smoothing her ruffled hide and drying her sweat. Then he mounted Jiminty.

"Didn't take him near as long that time," Joe said, grinning. "Might be hope for him yet."

Doyle snorted. "If we had a handful of years."

Doyle really doesn't like me, Andrew thought. *Doyle don't like much of anyone.* Glad it's not just me. Andrew wasn't used to people disliking him. Not only was he pretty easy-going, he was also the baseball team's star pitcher, so even though he played a lot of pranks with Chuck and Ed, everyone still liked him. Or at least pretended to like him. Doyle didn't pretend anything.

Charlie set a hard pace, and Andrew struggled to adjust to Jiminty's rhythm, which was totally different than Peppermint's. He couldn't believe he was doing this, riding with them, trying to figure out a way to fight that monstrous thing. He should be riding the other way. But that snake...and those people... He couldn't. He just couldn't.

When they switched horses again, Andrew had to concentrate to learn Dewmint's rhythm, but he soon discovered that her rhythm was totally smooth no matter how fast or slow she was going. In fact, she was so easy to ride, Andrew could almost see how horses caught on. For a moment he forgot about the snake and Pecos and just rode.

They rode through the remaining day and into the evening, only stopping to change horses. No one talked, not even Pecos, and whenever Andrew tried to ask him something, Pecos snapped *Shut up, boy; I'm tryin' to think!*

Left to his own thoughts, Andrew wondered about the dark voice Charlie had mentioned, the snake, the disappearing Grey Shaman, and Pecos. He didn't understand any of it, and he still didn't believe them. He didn't believe Pecos was more than a man. How could he be?

He wished he knew how to fight so he could help Pecos win, if it was even possible for Pecos to win. He wished he knew why he was here. He couldn't even mount a horse, but maybe that was the point. He was so totally useless someone thought he'd get Pecos killed, but Andrew wouldn't let that happen. He didn't want Pecos to die just because he sucked at everything.

He hadn't tried at anything in his entire life. He didn't bother trying, because he knew he'd fail. It just so happened he was incredibly good at baseball. And so he played baseball.

But now he had to try. He had to try because he was here and he shouldn't be. He had to try because somehow this wasn't a dream. It was real, and people were dying. He was going to learn to shoot and fight and kill things. And if he was terrible at it he'd just keep trying. He didn't want Pecos's death on his head. And if Pecos died, he'd be dead too, so he'd try for both of them.

When his mind got tired of trying to figure everything out, he thought about his mom and his body. Was his body still in his bed? Were his hands still holding that stupid book? Had it been more than a day there? Was he in a coma? What if some doctor declared him brain dead? Would his mom pull the plug on him? He shook his head in disgust. He had enough to worry about without making stuff up.

He thought about that moment when he'd decided to climb that enormous tree to shut Chuck up, to prove he wasn't a momma's boy. It all seemed so trivial now, so pointless. At the time a broken leg over summer vacation had seemed like the worst thing to ever happen. If he didn't count his dad never coming home. But now he knew better. This was the worst.

No matter what Charlie had said, those people had died because of Andrew. Andrew wasn't strong enough. He didn't know enough. He wasn't brave enough.

Every time he dismounted to switch horses he nearly fell flat on his face, but he didn't. He was so tired and so sore he could barely move, but they just kept riding. Riding and riding and riding. Andrew imagined a car, smiling wistfully as he thought they'd probably already be there, wherever there was. But no car appeared, and Andrew just got stiffer and sorer as the day went on.

As the last of the sun's rays vanished, Andrew urged Dewmint up beside Charlie. "Are we gonna stop soon?" he asked hopefully.

"Nope."

"We can't actually ride at night, can we?"

"Sure."

"How?"

"Horses see better than you."

Well that sucked. Andrew couldn't imagine staying in the saddle another minute, let alone the rest of the night. His bones ached. His head was hammering. He was hungry. He was thirsty. His hands were raw. His throat was coated in dust despite the bandana covering his mouth and nose. And he was scared. He was scared that even though they were riding away now, soon they'd be riding back towards that snake, that ridiculously, unbelievably huge snake, because apparently only one man could stop it, and Pecos was he.

I still say it's not really a snake, he thought. *What?* The snake thing. Not really a snake. It's more like a gnake, giant snake or mnake, monstrous snake. Never mind. Neither of those work. We'll just have to call it the really huge snake. *Boy...* Yeah? *I'm afraid you might be a bit touched in the head.* What? No, I mean...oh, never mind.

It was soon totally dark. So dark it felt like it was pressing down into Andrew, so dark he couldn't see past Dewmint's head, and he had to force himself to keep breathing. He'd never hated the dark more. It was stifling; and if he couldn't see, how the hell could Dewmint see? But Dewmint didn't trip once, didn't falter, didn't waver. She just kept running after Charlie, and when Charlie slowed, she slowed.

When they finally stopped again, Andrew hoped it was for the night, but it wasn't. He wearily removed the saddle from Dewmint and put it on Jiminty. Then they mounted and rode again.

Andrew adjusted to Jiminty's rhythm and tried to think of something, anything that would keep him awake. But he was so tired he just couldn't think. His eyes slipped closed and before he knew it Pecos was yelling, *Wake up, boy!* Andrew jerked upright, fumbling for the reins he'd dropped.

Sorry. I just...I'm not used to staying up so late. *You're such a sissy it pains me.* I'm not! I just... Crap. Maybe he was a sissy because if his mom showed up right that second, forced them to stop, made him cocoa, and tucked him into bed, he wouldn't complain. He shook his head. He wasn't a sissy. He'd prove it.

He peeled his eyes open and tried to focus on something, anything in the dark. But there was nothing to focus on, and he was soon lulled to sleep by the pounding of Jiminty's hooves. *Wake up!* Pecos yelled again, and Andrew's head snapped up. Sorry.

Pecos sighed. *Listen boy, how 'bout I tell you 'bout the time Joe and I rounded up three thousand head of cattle in one night?* Cattle? *I'm a rancher, boy.* What? Then why are you so gung-ho to fight this snake? *Somebody's gotta do it.* But...why you? *'Cause I can.* Andrew sighed. Pecos was either totally crazy or the strongest man alive if he thought he could actually fight that thing.

So is three thousand a lot? he asked, feeling more awake than he had in a while. Pecos snorted. *It is if they're ornery, wild Texas longhorns.* So what happened? Pecos started talking, and soon Andrew was sucked into the story. Pecos had a way of describing things so vividly Andrew felt like he was actually there watching Pecos wield his mighty rope. The others probably thought he was crazy, because they couldn't hear Pecos and every now and then Andrew burst out laughing. But it kept him awake, so Andrew didn't bother worrying about it.

When Pecos finished his story, Andrew asked him if the things Joe and the others had said about him were really true. *More or less.* More or less? *Sometimes more, sometimes less.* Andrew frowned. That wasn't really an answer, you know. What else have you done? *Well, there was this one time I had to deal with a pack of flesh weavers.* What the hell are flesh weavers? *I'm gettin' there, boy.* Maybe I don't wanna hear this story. *You do; it's a good one. So I was out in the desert...*

As the sky finally started to turn grey, even Pecos's stories couldn't keep Andrew awake. He kept slipping to one side or the other, jerking awake when Pecos snapped at him. When they stopped at dawn to switch horses, Andrew dismounted, stumbled, and fell into a heap on the ground.

"Better make some coffee, Doyle," Joe drawled, pulling Andrew to his feet. Andrew wearily dragged the saddle off Jiminty and wiped her down. Then he sat on the ground and promptly fell asleep.

A few minutes later Doyle woke him, shoving a steaming cup of tar into Andrew's hands. "Drink up, boy," he said roughly.

Andrew nodded blearily and took a sip. Damn! It was like getting punched in the head with a bulldozer! Doyle flipped some burnt biscuits out of a pan and handed Andrew a plate. Andrew wished there was something else to eat, but he wasn't going to ask

Doyle. Doyle scared him almost as much as the snake. Almost, but not quite.

He took a bite and choked it down, nearly spilling his coffee when the air shifted and the Grey Shaman sat beside him. "Damn it!" Andrew snapped. "Where did you come from?"

"Here, there. Somewhere," the shaman said, smiling widely. "How are things?"

You know damn well how things are. You did this, didn't you? Get this boy outta my body! Now! Folks're dyin'!

"Regrettably, there is nothing I can do about your current predicament."

Did you do this? Did you bring 'im here?

"What could I possibly have to gain by such an antic?"

Then why're you here? Pecos growled.

"I always enjoy a good conversation with you, but I do see Doyle made the coffee again. Andrew, a note, Doyle does not know the meaning of subtlety."

"Subtlety? What's that?" Andrew asked.

"Ah, Doyle, a pupil for you," the Grey Shaman said laughing, and just like that he was gone.

Andrew jumped again, staring at the empty space where the Grey Shaman had been. "How does he do that?" he gasped.

"Magic," Doyle growled. "Meddlin' old coot."

"Old? He doesn't look old at all! I mean his hair's grey, but he doesn't look any older than you or Joe."

"Legends say he walked these lands before the white man came," Charlie said. "But no one knows.

Grandmother met him when she was very young, and she says he has not changed."

"Wow...that's like...incredible," Andrew breathed. *Ain't incredible; it's annoyin'.* "Why's he called the Grey Shaman anyway? Why not just the shaman? Or his name or something?"

"No one knows his true name," Charlie said. "Grandmother says he's called Grey because he walks in the middle."

"What?"

"Neither black nor white, neither right nor wrong, neither good nor evil," Charlie explained with a shrug.

Andrew wasn't sure that was comforting. If you were dealing with someone, you'd like them to be on the side of right. *What's right?* You know, RIGHT. *Huh. I can say this, coyotes got a totally different sense of right than man.* What? Pecos didn't answer, so Andrew asked a different question. Whadda we do now? *What Joe said.* What'd Joe say? *You gotta get comfortable in my skin.* Andrew groaned. *Joe can get you ropin' this mornin'; then we ride.*

Andrew pinched himself one last time, knowing it wouldn't work, but still hoping. He didn't wake up, so he drained his coffee and stood. "Joe," he said with a sigh. "Pecos wants you to show me how to rope."

"Sure thing," Joe said as he stood. "Roping's a cinch."

Sure it is, Andrew thought as he followed Joe towards a clearing.

Joe pointed out a tall stump and said, "That'll work as our calf's head."

"Why a calf head?"

"Doesn't seem right to rope just a plain old stump," Joe said, ambling about twenty feet away.

"Don't you think we should be a bit closer?" Andrew asked.

"Nah, this'll work." Joe showed Andrew how his rope was tied to construct a loop. "See this bit here allows the rope to slide through. The loop should be pretty big, and once you've roped your calf, it'll tighten down small. The bigger the thing you're trying to rope, the bigger your loop needs to be to start."

Andrew nodded and watched as Joe whipped his rope over his head and started spinning it. Air rushed around Joe's head, until Andrew couldn't even see the loop anymore, just the edge of the rope as it spun by.

"Spin's ready, so I release. I just let the rope go." The rope sailed through the air and landed around the stump, and quick as quick, Joe had the loop pulled tight. "Don't want your calf to get away," he said, winking at Andrew. "Now you try."

It looked pretty easy, so Andrew took the rope and coiled it in his left hand the way Joe had done. He held the loop in his right hand, making sure the loop was nice and big, and then he raised his hand into the air and spun the rope. Only it didn't really spin. It flopped. And with every rotation it hit Andrew's head until it knocked his hat clean off.

"Get it higher," Joe said.

"I'm trying," Andrew growled.

"It's not so much in the wrist; use your arm more." Andrew tried to use his arm more, but when he did that the rope slipped down his body and he roped his feet. "Just your first try," Joe said agreeably. "Try again."

Andrew laughed. It was a horrible try. He really was very, very bad at this. If he was home he'd toss the rope in the trash and go play ball. But he wasn't, so he untangled his feet, untangled his rope, and tried again. This time, he managed to throw the rope, but it flew backwards instead of forwards.

"Bit different," Joe said casually. Andrew rolled his eyes and tried again. "You don't need to deliver hard," Joe said, adjusting Andrew's hand. "Roping's more of a finesse tool."

Andrew nodded, grinning when he finally managed to spin the rope without hitting his head, but when he released it, it sailed sideways and roped Joe. The next time the rope actually went towards the calf's head, but landed about ten feet shy.

"Why do I need to learn to rope anyway?" Andrew complained. "It's not like there're any cows around here. We're dealing with a snake, and it's way too big to be roped."

Joe smiled widely. "Rope's a versatile tool." He took the rope from Andrew, spun it, slipped the loop over Andrew's head, and pulled his feet out from under him before Andrew even knew what was happening. Andrew lay dazed on the ground for a moment, before pushing the rope off his feet and standing.

"That was pretty cool," he said grudgingly. "But I still don't see how that helps us."

Joe started spinning again, but this time he spun the loop in front of him, then flipped it into the air sideways, stepping through the loop, then spun the loop back into the air and roped Andrew's hat right off his head.

Andrew laughed. "Okay, I get it. Roping's cool, but shouldn't I be training to like, you know, actually fight the snake?" Andrew hated even saying those words, but he knew that's what Pecos wanted, what Pecos would do. And he knew he would eventually have to try. That snake was just going to keep following the road, destroying every town it came to, crushing men, women, and children, and there was a part of Andrew that couldn't deal with that. Someone had to stop it. And if it had to be Pecos, so be it.

Joe shrugged. "You never know what you'll need. Let's try some more."

Andrew rolled his eyes, but he took the rope from Joe and tried again. He tried throwing it like a baseball, but that didn't work. The loop just sailed through the air and got stuck in a tree. He tried throwing it like he cast his fishing line, but when he did that it went backwards again.

He threw for another hour or so, but he never managed to rope the calf. By the time they were done, his shoulder and arm ached horribly, and sometimes the calf head looked like two calf heads, maybe even three.

Finally, Andrew rolled up the rope and handed it to Joe. "I'm sorry; I just can't seem to get the hang of it."

"We'll try again," Joe said, and Andrew groaned.

He hated roping. It made him feel like a city slicker idiot. Pecos hadn't said anything while Andrew had been practicing, and Andrew was glad. He hoped Pecos had been thinking and not paying attention, because it was just too embarrassing. He'd never tried so hard to do anything before. But even trying hard he had failed. He gently rubbed his arm and shoulder. He'd trade his entire baseball card collection for an ice pack and some Advil. Hell. He'd trade everything he owned to be home.

Chapter Seven

I've got a plan, Pecos said suddenly. Yeah? Andrew thought, as he saddled Peppermint. He pulled himself into the saddle, relieved how much easier it already was, and started out after Charlie. Charlie had said they'd reach Grandmother's village in a few hours, and Andrew was glad it wouldn't be any longer. The coffee and roping lesson had revived him, but he wasn't sure how long he'd be able to ride without being lulled to sleep.

There's a story I heard once 'bout a rope made of pure gold that can hold anythin'. Who would make a rope out of gold? *Probably ain't real gold; just a story.* Okay? *Well, all we gotta do is find it and use it on that there snake.* But you just said it was just a story! *Yeah, but sometimes stories is real.* Andrew rolled his eyes. He couldn't believe Pecos's whole plan depended on a fictitious rope from a fictitious story. Do you at least know where it is? *Nope.* Swell. So how we gonna find it? *Charlie's grandma.* At least we're headed the right way.

You learn to rope? Um...Were you not watching? Andrew asked with a cringe. *Nope.* Well...yeah. *Yeah what?* It went. *Went how?* Um... Andrew tapped Peppermint into a gallop, that's what Pecos had said running fast but not outright running was called, and tried to think of a way to answer Pecos's question.

He wasn't used to anyone expecting anything from him. He was his mom's baby, so anything he did was good enough for her, even when he got C's on his report cards, and his dad had simply never asked anything from him. He might give Andrew a high five after he won a game or caught a fish, but he didn't have any expectations, not really.

Pecos actually wanted things from Andrew. He wanted Andrew to be good at all the things he was good at, but Andrew had only been here two days, and they had been riding most of the time. How could he be good at anything yet?

It went...badly, he thought finally. But Joe said we'd try again. *Humph.* I'm trying, Andrew thought desperately. *You shouldn't have to try. With my body you should be able to do anythin'! Can't you feel my power, my strength?* That doesn't even make sense. How could I feel your strength? *Try, boy! Try!* How?! I don't understand what you want from me!

There's strength in all of us. Well, duh, Andrew thought, rolling his eyes. *I mean beyond that, boy. Somethin' deeper. Somethin' that makes us more.* That's crazy. *It ain't. You can feel it, even see it. This strength is what makes me me. You have to use it; you have to harness it; you have to become me! It's the only way.*

Andrew sighed. There wasn't any way he'd ever be able to BE Pecos, not if Pecos really was who they said he was, but he closed his eyes, trusting Peppermint to follow Charlie, and tried to feel whatever it was Pecos was talking about. When his eyes were closed and he couldn't see Pecos's hands and legs, Pecos's body didn't feel all that different from his own. Andrew breathed deeply, trying to turn his eyes inward, trying to see what Pecos wanted him to see.

He didn't see anything. It was just dark. That same sort of rainbow dark it was when he closed his own eyes. And then all of the sudden, he felt it. A thrumming heat, a pulsing energy, right beneath the surface, just beyond his reach, humming, humming, humming. And out of the darkness a brilliant light shone, vibrant and golden. Andrew gasped and reached for it, but it slipped away, and the darkness returned.

"I saw it!" he said excitedly. *And?* Can't touch it. Pecos hissed angrily. *Should just be there! Part of you, me, US!* It isn't. It's...I don't know. I'm sorry. I'll keep trying. *Damn right you will.* I just said I would, didn't I? Pecos started muttering, and Andrew sighed. Life was so much simpler when no one wanted anything from him.

They rode hard for hours, and when Andrew wasn't trying to touch the thrumming strength inside Pecos, he watched the passing landscape. It was so different than anything he'd ever seen. The trees weren't tall here, just short scrubby things, some sort of evergreens, and there were lots of short cactuses and clumped cactuses, and a spikey plant Pecos called yucca.

He watched a weird little rodent creature stand on its hind legs. Pecos had said they were called prairie dogs, which made sense because they usually barked at

Andrew when he rode past. The one he was watching barked and scurried into its hole as a shadow passed overhead.

Andrew followed the shadow until it landed in a dead tree. His eyes widened when he saw it was an enormous black bird. The sun glinted off its black feathers and beak, and then suddenly it took flight again, spreading its vast wings, rising into the air, and casting a huge black shadow onto the ground.

What's that bird? Andrew asked, watching it in awe. *Huh? Oh, a raven.* It's amazing; look at it soar! *Just a bird.* Andrew rolled his eyes.

What's your real story, anyway? Andrew asked, hoping to distract himself from the problem of the snake. My mom used to tell me all kinds of stories, mostly fairy tales, but she likes you for some reason, so she used to tell me about you. I think she said you were raised by wolves. *Wolves?! Weren't raised by wolves.* Yeah, I didn't think a wolf could actually raise a human, but whadda I know? *Coyotes.* What? *Raised by coyotes.* Seriously? *What's wrong with that?* Nothing, I just...um...never mind.

Who ever heard of anyone being raised by coyotes? That was just weird. He frowned. Is that what Pecos had meant when he said one of his brothers had eaten all the eggs? Had he meant a coyote? Why would anyone call a coyote their brother? Maybe he really was dreaming. Andrew pinched himself, just to check, but he didn't wake up. He'd known he wouldn't. It was real. And if it was real, that meant Pecos had been raised by coyotes. Andrew shook his head and focused on the changing landscape.

Huge, red rocks rose out of the earth, breaking the ground, stretching towards the blue sky, making Andrew feel tiny. They rode through the rocks down into a sheltered valley filled with adobe huts spread out in a circle with a huge green space in the middle. Children were running through the grassy circle, chasing hoops and shrieking with laughter.

Charlie slowed to a walk, dismounting just at the edge of the village. He walked into the village, nodding at the men who were there and stopping in front of one of the larger huts. An ancient looking woman stood in front of it, gnarled hands wrapped around the top of a carved wooden staff, eyes white with blindness.

Charlie spoke softly as he gave the old woman a gentle hug. She smiled broadly at him, white teeth bright against her dark, wrinkled skin, speaking cheerfully in a lilting language Andrew couldn't understand before turning towards Andrew. In spite of her obvious blindness, Andrew knew she could see him; her eyes felt like they were piercing his very soul.

"This is a surprise," she said in English. "I expected Pecos, but I did not expect you, boy. Who are you? How did you come here?"

Andrew's mouth dropped open. How did everyone know he wasn't Pecos? Charlie, the Grey Shaman, Charlie's Grandma. Was he wearing some kind of sign?

He smiled awkwardly and said, "Name's Andrew Rufus, ma'am." He may be a momma's boy, but never let it be said he was a rude momma's boy. "And I don't know how I got here. Maybe a book I was reading? Maybe magic? I don't know."

"Interesting." Andrew fought not to roll his eyes; his mom hated it when he rolled his eyes, so he figured Charlie's Grandma might not like it either. "Come inside," she said, and Andrew followed her into her hut, surprised when the others stayed outside.

"Sit, Andrew, sit," she said, gesturing towards a low bench.

Andrew sat; mind still spinning. How did everyone know he wasn't Pecos? Didn't that make it seem like it really was a dream? Like everyone was really him and that's how they knew? He grasped at the thought, feeling as if he was clinging to the very last remnant of his sanity, but he couldn't hold it. It slipped away as soon as her next words broke through his thoughts.

"This is no dream." Andrew gasped, but she went on. "Some force, I know not what or who, brought you here," she said intently. "Powerful forces are clashing against each other, changing reality, changing everything. You and Pecos are part of it."

"Why?" Andrew asked doubtfully. Pecos he could understand, but him? He was nobody, nothing, just a kid.

"Your part in this matters," she said firmly. "In spite of Pecos's strength, his power, his commitment to do right, you are very important. You can affect reality, existence, life."

Andrew felt the blood drain from his face, and cold washed over him. He didn't want to affect anything. He didn't want to matter. He didn't want that weight on his shoulders. He wanted to go home. "Can you send me home?" he gasped.

"No; that power is not mine. It takes a very powerful..." she paused searching for a word. "Witch...to create such magic. Time is delicate. So delicate. Like a blade of grass or a flower; here and gone."

Andrew swallowed hard, wishing he was home, wishing he'd been able to hold onto the hope that it was a dream for more than a second. "How did you know I'm not from this time?"

"Your eyes." His eyes? What did that mean? "Have you met Septimis?" she asked abruptly.

"Who's that?"

"The father of snakes."

"Oh. I wouldn't say we met, but I did see him."

"The very breath of darkness whispered in his ear and angered him. But what the dark is seeking is not the same as Septimis."

"I heard a voice," Andrew said softly. "In my dream. I heard it tell him that his children were treated badly, trampled underfoot, their corpses used to make belts and boots."

She nodded her head. "That is what I saw also. Take care. The dark is hungry. Waiting to feast on power, power so raw, so pure, it will never have to hide again."

"What does that mean?" Andrew whispered, heart hammering.

"I do not know. Why have you come?"

"Right." Um, why did we come, Pecos? *Ask her 'bout the rope.* "Pecos wants me to ask you about a golden rope. He says it can hold anything."

She rocked back and forth. "Yes, the Stone Rope."

"Um, no, Pecos said it was gold."

"Yes, the Stone Rope."

Andrew waited for her to continue, but she said nothing. "Go on, please," he said.

"What do you want to know?"

"Where can we find the rope?" Andrew asked. "Will it hold the snake?"

"Many years ago there was a lovely young woman who loved a warrior from another tribe. Their fathers were enemies, but the woman yearned to have the heart of the warrior as her own. The warrior, however, did not see the woman. His heart was bound on making his father proud. So the woman braided together long strands of gilded moonlight. It took her many seasons. She foolishly believed if she caught the warrior, he would belong to her, and so she used the rope to trap him. The shame of capture caused the young warrior to turn to stone. The woman wept a river of tears, and the river swept both of them into the sea."

Well that's super depressing, Andrew thought. Also pretty ridiculous. Moonlight? *Shut up, boy! Ask her where it is!* "Um...so do you know where it is?"

"Many tried to use the rope, but there was no warrior strong enough to wield it. The woman's father tried to destroy it, but it could not be destroyed, so he asked Grandfather Bear to keep it."

"Who's Grandfather Bear?" Andrew asked, dreading the answer. "Is he a real bear? He's not like Septimis, is he?" Andrew couldn't imagine a bear the size of Septimis.

"No," she replied. "He is not the first. He is second or third; I do not know. But he is very old, massive, dangerous, and very clever. He hates man. The tribe knew he would keep the rope from man. And in doing so, he would keep it from causing more harm."

Andrew popped his knuckles nervously. "Hates man? Why?"

She shrugged her shoulder delicately. "That is Grandfather Bear's story, not mine."

"What?"

"Why he hates man. The story belongs to Grandfather Bear."

Andrew had no idea what that meant. How could a story belong to anyone? "Massive, huh? Like what're we taking here? The size of a car?"

"A car?"

"Um, you know, a wagon."

"Oh, yes, he is easily as tall as a wagon is long. Maybe taller." She gestured towards the roof. "I saw him only once when I was much younger. His eyes glow like embers, his claws are long as trout, and his strength flattens trees."

Maybe Andrew had never really had a bad day, not until today. This was a bad day. All those other days he'd thought were bad, they were like little hiccups.

The father of snakes decimating towns and eating people; a massive bear who hated men for some reason only he knew. It just got worse and worse.

"The Stone Rope is heavy and long," she added. "Only a man of incredible strength can wield it. Pecos could, but I do not know about you. You are just a boy."

Andrew gulped. This was not good. Just one more thing Pecos could do that he couldn't. Not only was he not strong enough, he was terrible at roping. "Maybe Joe can do it; he's super good at roping."

She looked doubtful. "Perhaps."

Andrew stood awkwardly. "I guess that's it. Thank you…um ma'am."

"You may call me Grandmother," she said with a grin.

"Really? Cool. Thanks, Grandma. I…we appreciate it."

"Pecos is a wild and untamed river. Do not fight him."

"I'm not; I mean, I'm trying to work with him. I don't know how to do what he wants me to do…I'm not him!"

"You will learn," she said, leading him to the doorway; but she stopped suddenly, grabbing his arm. Her eyes glowed; her voice was dark. "Pecos, beware. A black shadow crosses the sun. It follows you; it watches you. It hates." She blinked, and her eyes were sightless once more.

"What does that mean?" Andrew whispered.

"I do not know. I only saw a bottomless shadow." She shivered. "Be careful."

Andrew nodded, wishing he was home, and stepped outside.

"So?" Doyle asked.

"I guess we have to visit Grandfather Bear. Oh crap, I forgot to ask her where he lives."

"I know," Charlie said. "But we must wait until morning."

Andrew almost cried with relief. He was so tired he could barely stand, his vision was blurry, and his leg muscles were shaking. *Sissy,* Pecos muttered. *Didn't I tell you 'bout that time I rode for five days straight to catch them rustlin' thieves?* Andrew rolled his eyes, ignoring Pecos, and followed Charlie out of the village and into a meadow just beyond.

"We'll camp here," Charlie said.

Andrew couldn't wait to sleep. He stripped the saddle off Jiminty in record time, rubbed down all three horses, then wrapped the saddle blanket up like a pillow and dropped to the ground. As soon as he closed his eyes, Doyle kicked him in the ribs.

"What?" Andrew gasped, holding his side.

"Got work to do."

"What work? I rubbed down my horses!"

"Gotta learn to use your guns," Doyle snarled. "Ain't much use if you can't even fight."

Andrew missed home, where his only chore was picking up his clothes off the floor. "I'm so tired I can't even see straight," he complained. "Can't I take a nap first?"

Doyle snorted in disgust. "This one time Pecos and I rode for five days straight!"

"So I've been told. Is that a 'no'?"

"Yes!"

"Yes, it's a no? Or yes, I can have a nap?"

"Yes it's a no! And NO you can't have a nap!"

"Best make the boy some coffee so he doesn't shoot you," Joe said chuckling.

"Fine," Doyle snapped, and Andrew almost laughed. Coffee was their answer to everything.

"Pecos told me not to touch his guns," Andrew said, sitting beside the fire. Doyle snorted, and Pecos growled, *Changed my mind, boy. You're a walkin' disgrace.* Andrew sighed deeply, wishing his dad had been into hunting or something so Andrew wouldn't look like a complete idiot. He'd never held a gun in his life, unless you counted water guns, which he didn't think they would. He drank three cups of thick coffee before following Doyle further away from the village towards a small hill.

"We'll shoot at that hill right there."

"Just a bunch of dirt," Andrew said. "How will I be able to tell what I'm shooting at?"

Doyle glared at him. "You complain a lot, boy."

"What?! I don't complain! I haven't complained about riding all day or working like a dog. I'm just tired, and I don't understand how I'm gonna tell where the bullet went. Don't we need a target or something?"

Doyle snarled, and Andrew backed away. Doyle was scary. *Ain't scary; well, he is, but...well hell.* That did NOT make me feel better, Andrew snapped. *You do complain a lot.* I don't!

"We'll stand this log up," Doyle said grudgingly.

"Thank you," Andrew muttered.

"Don't thank me, boy!" Doyle snapped, walking a good fifty feet away and propping the log against the side of the hill.

"So what, just point and shoot?" Andrew asked when Doyle got back.

"City slicker," Doyle muttered. "I just hope you don't shoot Pecos's foot off. See here, this is how a gun works." Doyle began to slowly and carefully show Andrew each part of Pecos's gun, telling him how the parts worked as he went. Then he made Andrew repeat the names and functions.

"Today use your right hand," he said when he had finished. "If you're adequate, we'll work on your left hand later."

Andrew tried to imagine the look on his mom's face if he told her he'd shot one gun, let alone two guns at once. She'd ground him for life. She hated guns, swords, knives, pretty much anything that could kill someone, and violence, all violence. She firmly believed that everyone should just get along. She would hate the real Pecos Bill.

"You've got six shots before you need to reload," Doyle continued. "Flip the cylinder open, eject the cartridges, and put fresh ones in." Doyle quickly drew and shot. At first Andrew thought Doyle had missed, but he had shot a twig off the side of the log and as it flew into the air, he unloaded five more shots into it, reloaded, and shot it six more times. When it finally landed, it was just wood dust.

Andrew blinked. "Wow! That was REALLY fast! And accurate. I mean that stick is GONE!"

"I ain't as fast as Pecos," Doyle said.

Andrew couldn't believe that. He couldn't imagine anyone being faster than Doyle. Doyle handed the empty gun to Andrew. "Aim it a few times, draw it a few times, pull the trigger, just see how it feels in your hand."

Andrew put the gun into his holster. Then he drew it, aimed at the log, and pulled the trigger. He repeated this action over and over. "It feels okay I guess."

"Go ahead and load it." Andrew took his time, pulling each cartridge out of his belt and placing it carefully into the gun. He closed the cylinder, made sure the hammer wasn't back, and placed the gun back in his holster. He hoped this wasn't going to be like roping. He hoped he didn't shoot himself.

"Now draw, pull the hammer back, aim for the log, and fire. Don't flinch; that'd pull your gun sideways."

"Why would I flinch?"

"Some do." Doyle said and motioned to go ahead.

Andrew drew, cocked, aimed, and fired. The ground next to the log exploded. "Was that okay?" he asked, bummed he hadn't hit the log.

Doyle actually grinned. "Pretty damn good for your first try. Again." Andrew fired five more times, and each time he hit the ground next to the log.

He reloaded and hit the log once. Sweet! I like this better than roping anyway, he thought. *You would.*

Takes a real man to rope; any ol' fool can shoot a gun. Andrew rolled his eyes. He kept practicing for a while and did better each time. He couldn't believe how patient Doyle was; he wasn't snarling or snapping, and once he even laughed. He was almost…pleasant.

"That's enough for today," Doyle grunted once the sun was low in the sky.

Andrew sighed in relief. Shooting was fun, but he was so tired and Pecos was so heavy. *You're doin' it again.* What? *Complainin'!* Andrew rolled his eyes, picked up his empty cartridges, and headed back towards camp, feeling more cheerful than he had in days. It was such a relief to finally be good at something.

Chapter Eight

As they were walking, Andrew heard shouts and turned to see a group of men striding outside the village. They were yelling, pushing another man as they went, but then the man fell to the ground and the others began kicking him.

"What're they doing?" asked Andrew.

"Don't know," Doyle replied.

"Shouldn't we stop them?"

"Nah."

"But they're ganging up on that guy!"

"They got their own justice," Doyle said, shrugging and continuing on towards the campfire.

Andrew started to follow Doyle, but he couldn't. He'd counted, and it was ten against one. What kind of justice could that be? The kind that wasn't fair; that's what kind. Andrew started running towards them, intent on stopping them. *What're you doin', boy?* Pecos snapped. That man needs help. It's like ten to one. *Stay out of it!* Pecos said firmly.

"Hey!" Andrew yelled. "Stop it!"

One of the warriors turned towards Andrew. "Walk away, White Man," he snarled.

"No!" Andrew said, grabbing one of the men and pulling him away from the fallen man. "You don't just gang up on someone like that. It's not right!"

The men stopped kicking and stared at Andrew. "What do you know of right?" the first warrior demanded. "You steal our land and murder our people."

"I haven't done any of that," Andrew sputtered. *Walk away, boy. This ain't gonna end well.* Andrew gulped, fear pushing forward, but he'd come too far; he couldn't back down now. He couldn't leave that man on the ground, bloody and broken.

"Leave him alone," he ordered.

The tallest man stepped forward. "I know of you. You are just a boy in a man's body," he mocked, lunging towards Andrew, hands outstretched.

Andrew jumped to the side and swung his fist. Pain shot up his arm as his knuckles connected with the man's cheek. "Crap! That hurts!" he hissed. *Can't even throw a punch. I'll let Doyle skin you if you break anythin'!* Not now, Pecos! Andrew ducked another punch and tackled one of the men. He rolled off, jumping to his feet, fists up. He had no idea what he was doing. Everything was happening so fast, but at least he was still on his feet. The men started towards him as one, and Andrew backed away.

Can't run now. You started it; you finish it. But how? *One punch at a time.* They rushed him, and Andrew punched one man in the face, ducked a hit, slammed his elbow into something soft and punched again, but there were just too many of them. He shielded his face and rammed with his shoulder, but suddenly he was on the ground, and they were on top of him, raining blows on his ribs and head.

But then the blows stopped. Andrew lay cringing, waiting for another hit, but it never came, so he peeked through his hands. The village men were scattered on the ground moaning, and Doyle, Charlie, and Joe stood over Andrew.

"You alright, boy?" Joe asked, offering him a hand.

Andrew's cheeks burned. He really wished he hadn't been curled up in a ball. *Curled in a ball?! What the hell's wrong with you?!* Sorry, I just...anyway. Andrew gasped as Joe pulled him to his feet. "How's the face?" Andrew asked worriedly. "Pecos's gonna be mad if I messed up his face." *Damn right I will!*

Joe laughed. "You look the same to me."

"Great..." Andrew limped toward the man he'd tried to protect. "Are you okay?"

The man kicked at him. "Stay away from me, you filthy white man!"

"What?! But...I mean..." *Told you not to meddle.* Shut up, Pecos.

The man rolled to his knees and started trying to crawl away from the village, but one of the warriors jumped up, grabbed the man by his shirt, and pulled him back, yelling in the same language Grandma had spoken. Andrew watched, confused. He'd thought he was doing the right thing, but maybe he hadn't been.

The tall warrior approached Andrew. "You have a heart of courage," he said. "This man is evil; he must die."

"Die?" Andrew gasped.

"The council demands his blood," he said with a shrug. Then he held out his hand and grinned widely.

Andrew was totally confused, but he shook the man's hand, knowing it would be an insult not to. The man nodded and walked away, towards the condemned man.

Andrew turned back towards camp. He didn't want to see what happened next. He supposed a council probably wasn't any different than a jury. What they were doing had seemed terrible and wrong, but now he wasn't sure.

"We all fight for what we think's right," Doyle said, walking beside Andrew. "But not everybody's right is the same. And sometimes, what you think is right, ain't."

"Then how do you know when to fight?"

Doyle shrugged. "You just do, like you did. Why did you?"

Why had he? He'd never been in a fight before. He'd never wanted to be in a fight. At school when he saw someone getting bullied, he just looked the other way and kept walking. But not today. Why not today?

He'd thought he could save him. He hadn't been able to save any of those people from Septimis, but he'd thought maybe, just maybe, he could save one guy from ten. What had he been thinking? He didn't know how to fight. He hadn't won, and he hadn't saved anyone. That man was going to die. In all likelihood he had done something to deserve it, but even if he hadn't, Andrew couldn't save him.

"Not sure," he finally mumbled.

"Well, now you've been in a fistfight," Doyle said, slapping Andrew on the back.

Andrew stumbled but caught himself before he fell on his face. "That's true! Chuck and Ed're gonna be so jealous! They've never been in a real fight. It was kinda incredible! I don't know if Pecos's body took over or what, but I just sorta moved when I needed to. I felt invincible for just a second."

Doyle chuckled. "Pretty sure that was all you, kid."

"Why's that?"

"Pecos would've crushed 'em in a minute flat."

Damn straight. "Come on, really?"

"Seen 'im do it."

"So Pecos could have beaten all ten guys, all on his own?"

"Easy."

"Could you?"

"Sure; just take me a bit longer."

It was incredible, unbelievable really, but Andrew was beginning to believe they really could do everything they said they could. *I've been tellin' you all along.* "Would you teach me to fight?" he asked.

Doyle raised an eyebrow. "You wanna fight me?"

"Well," Andrew stuttered. "Not for real." For some reason Doyle didn't seem as scary as he had before. He was still scary, terrifying in fact, but Andrew didn't mind as much. He kind of liked that he was riding around with one of the scariest looking dudes he'd ever seen.

Doyle grinned his wide, wolfish grin and said, "Sure, when we got time. Now let's eat."

Andrew sat by the fire and touched his face gingerly, groaning softly. It didn't hurt when I was fighting them, he thought. But everything sure hurts now. Pecos chuckled. *You don't feel much when you're in it. Pain comes afterwards.* That sucks. *If it hurt when they hit, you would've run. This way you stood and fought like a man. Sorta. 'Cept for that bit at the end.* Andrew flushed. He hadn't meant to roll into a ball; he'd just been trying to protect himself.

His ribs were tender, but nothing was broken. Charlie cleaned his knuckles with water and slathered a white cream over them. "Honey paste," he said. "Grandmother makes it. You'll heal faster." Then he wrapped Andrew's hands with clean strips of cloth.

When Charlie had finished, Doyle handed Andrew a plate of cooked meat and burnt biscuits and a steaming cup of coffee. *Ah, coffee.* Can you taste it? Andrew asked in surprise. *Huh?* I mean, I'm running your body and eating and what not. I can taste it. I can feel pain. Can you? *I feel, taste, and hear everythin' you do.* Andrew frowned. That sucks. Sorry 'bout the fight then. Everything still really smarts. *It smarts 'cause you're such a sissy.* Never mind, Andrew snapped. I'm not sorry at all.

Joe played a sad sounding song on his harmonica, and Andrew leaned back on the ground, watching the stars overhead. Even with the fire, the stars were brighter than he'd ever seen them at home. A shooting star whistled by, leaving a fleeting trail of gold. A day ago, he would have wished to go home, but today he just watched it fly.

There was something about this place. Something he couldn't quite grasp. It was so real, so vibrant, so alive; it made the real world or the future world seem pale in comparison. He missed his mom. He missed her cooking a lot. And he hoped he wasn't stuck here forever. But right now? Right this moment? It was all right. Everything was all right.

Charlie started telling a story about his great-great grandfather and Grandfather Bear, and Andrew leaned forward so he could hear every word. He still couldn't believe there could be a snake as gigantic as Septimis or a bear as big as a car. He was NOT looking forward to meeting him.

"Grandfather eventually escaped," Charlie finished. "And when he returned, the council said that no one from the village could cross into Grandfather Bear's woods again."

Joe whistled. "He sounds like a bad one."

"Wait; aren't we going into his woods?" Andrew asked.

"Yep," Charlie said.

Andrew gulped. *He's just a bear,* Pecos snorted. *Nothin' scary 'bout bears.* Nothing scares you; you grew up with coyotes. I've never even seen a coyote. Or a bear, well except in the zoo, but I don't think that counts. *City slicker.*

Andrew cleared his throat and told the others what Grandma had said. They didn't seem surprised. How can they not be scared? *Why bother bein' scared?* I don't know…'cause…Oh, never mind.

Andrew sighed and turned his back to the fire. He'd never been so tired in his entire life. His hands and ribs ached, and his right arm hurt so bad from all the roping practice and shooting he was surprised he could even move it. But in spite of the pain and the cold, hard ground he fell asleep in a minute.

He dreamed of soft pillows, kisses on his forehead, and fists flying towards his face. He dreamed of screaming children, dying men, and snakes eating bears and bears eating snakes.

Charlie shook him awake before the sun had even risen, and Andrew stumbled groggily to his feet, wishing Charlie had a snooze button. He groaned as he walked forward and paused to stretch. Charlie joined him, copying Andrew's motions.

"You should feel that stretch in the back of your legs," Andrew explained.

"I do," Charlie said, nodding.

Quit this sissy stretchin' stuff. Charlie likes it. *What's Charlie know?* Andrew laughed and finished stretching. Then he saddled Dewmint and mounted up, following Charlie as he rode into the tree-covered hills.

"This isn't light," Andrew muttered. "This is pre-light; no, pre-pre-light." *This's late! I'd had you all up ages ago.* I'm glad you're not in charge then. *Whadda you mean I'm not in charge? Who do you think's runnin' things? It ain't you, city boy!* Someone's grumpy this morning. *Well, it ain't me!*

Andrew rolled his eyes. Pecos certainly didn't like it when things didn't go his way, but Andrew was used to it. Things never went his way unless he was standing on the pitcher's mound. He grinned, thinking about Pecos spending a day or two inside Andrew's body.

"Sore?" Joe asked, bringing his horse up beside Andrew's.

"Bit. Face hurts."

"I remember my first fight."

"How old were you?"

Joe chuckled. "Seventeen. It was with Pecos."

"Really?" Andrew asked in surprise. "You fought Pecos?"

"Sure did. Didn't win."

Andrew laughed. "To hear you guys tell it, no one could win against Pecos."

"Never seen a man yet who could beat Pecos or even a group of men. Once saw him fight what must have been a hundred men and come out on top."

"No way." Andrew wasn't that gullible. He could accept that Pecos was different, stronger, faster than most men, but a hundred men? No way he could swallow that line.

"It's true."

Andrew frowned, looking for any sign that Joe was kidding, but he didn't see any. Joe completely believed what he was saying. "How'd he get to be this way?" Andrew asked.

"Don't know. Just is."

Andrew frowned, but Pecos spoke up, *I done told you, boy. It's the strength, the power.* Andrew closed his eyes as he had before and looked. If he was quiet, if he allowed his mind to drift, he could feel it, could see it, bright and golden, humming along Pecos's body, part of Pecos, all of Pecos, but Andrew still couldn't touch it. Every time he reached for it, it jumped away and disappeared.

So it's like this for everyone? *Don't know. Maybe some don't use it at all. Maybe some only use it a bit. Maybe it doesn't even work the same.* Does Joe have it? *You seen the man rope?* Charlie? Pecos chuckled. *I could lose a whisker hair in a forest, and he'd be able to find it.* Huh. What about Doyle? *You'd probably rather not know.* Andrew shuddered, hoping he never found out. So how come I've never seen it or felt it? *I don't know how things are in your time. I'm just tellin' you how it is here.*

Andrew tried to focus on it, this strength, this power inside Pecos, but the harder he looked, the more he lost it. He finally quit trying and looked around him. He hadn't realized they had left the short trees behind and were now riding through an evergreen forest with tall pines stretching towards the sky, the rising sun turning their green needles golden.

Birds swooped through the branches calling to each other; squirrels chattered back and forth. There were animals everywhere. Andrew had never seen so much life in a forest, but the further they rode, the quieter everything grew. The horses' hooves made no sound; there were no birds, no chatter of woodland creatures. It was so quiet, so eerie, it gave Andrew the creeps.

"We oughta make some noise," Charlie said. "Let Grandfather Bear know we ain't tryin' to sneak up on 'im."

Chapter Nine

Andrew fervently wished they were headed anywhere else. Well, except back towards Septimis. He supposed this creepy forest was better than that. *Why you gotta be such a sissy? You'd think after your fight you'd man up a bit.* Andrew snorted. He was beginning to realize he'd never be able to live up to Pecos's expectations. He wasn't sure why he was even trying to; especially since he knew he was going to fail.

Because no one else was making any noise and he didn't want to startle a massive, angry, man-hating bear Andrew started singing. "Take me out to the ballgame, take me out to the crowd, buy me some peanuts and cracker jacks, I don't care if I never come back!" It sounded really strange in Pecos's voice, and Andrew wondered if Pecos ever sang.

No one told him to stop, so he kept going. "Let me root, root..." Andrew stuttered to a stop as they rounded a curve and a dark, massive cave mouth came into view. Nothing green grew near the mouth, and it was surrounded by piles of gleaming, white bones. Dewmint halted without Andrew even touching the reins and stepped backwards twice before stopping completely.

There wasn't a sound to be heard, and the cave was so dark it seemed to suck the light right out of the sky.

Andrew's heart thudded madly when he saw a human skull lying among the bones.

"I'm not going in there," he whispered. *You gotta.* Why? *Can't send one of the others.* Why not? *What if he ate 'em? Which one would you pick?* Andrew started to say Doyle, but he couldn't. They'd all been...nice. They hadn't left him behind, they'd taken breaks when they wouldn't have, they'd given him bone-warming coffee, they'd taught him, and they hadn't yelled or been angry when he hadn't done well.

"You've gotta be kidding me," Andrew hissed. Why can't the bear come out? *If you can get 'im to come out, great, if not...* How am I gonna talk to this bear anyway? I mean, it's a BEAR. *He talks.* He whats? *He talks. Some do.* No way! Do any of your horses talk? Pecos chuckled. *Course not.* But why not? *Just don't.*

Charlie and the others were looking at Andrew expectantly. It was hard to remember that he was both Andrew and Pecos. Pecos was their leader, so even though they couldn't hear him, they trusted that Pecos was there, speaking. Andrew grinned crookedly, trying to still his shaking hands. "Pecos says we'll, um...he and I...will, um...take care of this."

"You sure?" Joe asked, grin absent for once.

"Sure I'm sure," Andrew croaked, dismounting, relieved when he did it rather well. "Don't I seem sure?" *Quit babblin', boy!* Sorry. Andrew tried to grin but flinched as he stepped forward. I'm so stiff I can't even walk straight. *Your own fault. If you'd just get out of the way and let my body take charge.* I know, I know.

Andrew walked towards the cave mouth slowly, stepping over and around the piled and strewn about bones, ignoring the damp smell of death and the oddly dark color of the dirt. Several feet from the cave entrance, he paused and called out, "Grandfather Bear? Are you there?" A low growl echoed from inside. "I'm not...I mean...I've come to ask you a question," Andrew said shakily. "Would you come out?"

"No..." a hard, gravelly voice replied. "You come in."

Andrew really, really, really did not want to do that. He thought about pulling his gun, but he didn't want Grandfather Bear to think he was trying to hurt him. He stepped forward a couple feet then stopped. It was so dark in the cave he wouldn't be able to see; what if the bear tried to eat him? Suddenly a light flashed, and a small fire bloomed to life deep within. So he talks AND makes fire? *Looks like.* But he's a bear? *Yep.* You sure? *Yep.* You've seen him? *Yep.* He's big? *Yep.*

Andrew inched inside the cave, dreading being mauled to death or eaten alive. He walked slowly down the passageway, until he could see a shadow just beyond the fire, a huge shadow, a shadow that moved, and he realized it wasn't a shadow at all. It was Grandfather Bear.

Grandfather Bear turned to face Andrew and stretched his long arms towards the ceiling. His enormous claws scraped the roof, and Andrew stepped back in horror. He was huge! Taller and wider than a car or a truck. Just...huge! Grandfather Bear yawned, and his mouth opened so wide Andrew was sure he could eat all of him in three quick bites. Maybe only two.

"Your singing is awful," the bear growled. "Woke me from a dead sleep."

Andrew gasped and flushed at the same time. "I'm sorry," he stuttered, totally in awe. He was talking to a bear. A bear! "We didn't want you to think we were trying to sneak up on you."

"As if you could," he snorted. "My patience fades, and you look tasty; why are you here?"

Andrew's hand fluttered towards his gun, but he stopped himself. *Couldn't draw fast enough anyway.* Not helping, Pecos. "We came to ask you about the Stone Rope. The father of all snakes is killing people, and we need to stop him."

"Septimis has risen?" the bear said in some surprise. "I have been asleep." He stretched again, scraping the roof of the cave so hard, sparks flew towards Andrew. Andrew held himself still, trying not to flinch.

"And why should I care, human child?"

Human child? "How do you...but..." How did he know? How could he tell?

"I propose a trade," Grandfather Bear said. "I have not laughed in hundreds of years." He lumbered closer to Andrew, so close Andrew could see his large, glowing, amber eyes. "What is there to laugh about, yes?" He shrugged. "If you can make me laugh, child, I will give you the rope. If however, you fail," he grinned widely, sharp teeth glinting. "I will strip the flesh from your bones."

That ain't a real good deal. You don't say. Andrew wanted to run. He wanted to run out of the cave screaming, jump onto Dewmint, and ride until he was so far away from Grandfather Bear and Septimis he didn't feel scared anymore. But he knew... And this was annoying because why did he care? When had he grown a conscience? He knew he'd never outride the guilt.

"Okay," Andrew whispered. *Okay?! You outta your mind?! You let that bear eat me, and I'm gonna...I don't know what!*

"Well?" Grandfather Bear growled.

In spite of the fire, the darkness pressed down on Andrew, and his breath came fast and hard. How could he make an ancient bear laugh? What would he even think was funny? Andrew thought of all those people crushed alive by Septimis; he thought of their screams and their desperation. Then he suddenly remembered what Chuck had told him once when they were lost in the woods, and he grinned.

"Okay, so these two kids are walking through the woods one day when a vicious, scary bear steps out from the trees." *What you doin'? Tryin' to make 'im mad?* Shut up, Pecos. "The first kid bends down and tightens his shoe laces. The other kid says 'What're you doing? You'll never outrun that bear!' The first kid smiles and says, 'I know, but all I have to do is outrun you.'"

The words fell onto the cave floor, and silence filled the air. Andrew held his breath, waiting, hoping. Pecos was yelling at him, but Andrew ignored him, staring across the fire at Grandfather Bear.

A sound like rocks scraping together filled the cave, growing louder and louder, and Andrew gasped with relief. Grandfather Bear was laughing. He was actually laughing! Andrew wasn't going to die, at least not right this second. *Well I'll be damned.*

"Only have to outrun YOU!" the bear laughed loudly. "Well done, human child. Well done." He turned, disappearing into the back of the cave, and when he reappeared he was carrying a gleaming rope in his paws. "Take it; it has never done me any good," he said, tossing the rope towards Andrew. "You will not be able to wield it, but it is yours." The rush of air put out the fire, tossing sparks and casting the cave into darkness except for the eerie glow of the rope.

"Now go..." Grandfather Bear growled. "Before I change my mind!"

"Thank you," Andrew gasped, jumping for the rope. He grabbed it and pulled, but it was so heavy it didn't even budge. *Hurry, boy!* I'm trying! He wrapped both hands around the rope and ripped, but it barely moved. Andrew bit his lip, trying to use Pecos's strength, trying to channel Pecos's power. He grunted, pulling, and managed to drag the rope from the cave one step at a time.

He dropped to his knees in relief when he felt the sun on his face. A shudder ran through him, and he realized he was freezing. He lifted his face to the sun, letting it soak into his skin, trying to halt the shaking of his body, trying to breathe.

I can't believe that worked, Pecos muttered. Andrew didn't respond. He was trying not to vomit. He wanted away from Grandfather Bear's cave as quickly as possible, but he couldn't feel his legs, and his heart was beating so hard his chest hurt.

The rope had fallen in front of him, and Andrew stared at it. It glowed in the sunlight, reflecting light like a strand of mirrors. Andrew could almost believe it was made from moonlight. Almost. He touched it gingerly. It was smooth under his fingers, like glass, thinner than Pecos's rope, but there were so many coils. How long do you think it is? *Hopefully just long enough.* What? *Get movin', boy!*

Charlie pulled Andrew to his feet and between the two of them they managed to drag the Stone Rope over to Peppermint. They heaved it upward, hanging it over the saddle horn. Peppermint nickered with distress, and Charlie frowned.

"Gonna need to get some more horses. You can't ride with the rope; too heavy," he said.

"I can't ride bareback," Andrew said worriedly. He was sure Pecos could ride bareback, backwards, and upside down if he wanted to, but Andrew struggled just to stay in the saddle.

"Take my saddle," Charlie said. "We'll get a new one in the village."

Andrew took Charlie's saddle, saddled Jiminty, and mounted. We got the rope; now what? he asked Pecos. *Village first.*

"To the village," Andrew said. Charlie nodded and turned his horse back the way they'd come. Andrew glanced at the cave one more time and shuddered. He hoped he never, ever, ever saw Grandfather Bear again.

"Is he as big as they say?" Joe asked, riding beside Andrew.

Andrew cringed. "Bigger."

"How'd you convince him to give you the rope?"

"I didn't. He suggested a trade."

"A trade?"

"Yeah. He said if I could make him laugh, he'd let me have the rope, and if I didn't…he'd eat me."

"Bad deal."

"That's what Pecos said."

"So?"

"I made him laugh." Andrew tried to forget the part where he had imagined Grandfather Bear's claws ripping the flesh from his face and eating it. He tried to forget the terror he'd felt right up until the moment Grandfather Bear had laughed.

Joe didn't ask any more questions, and they rode silently back towards the village. *Stop here,* Pecos commanded when they reached the spot they'd camped the night before.

"Pecos wants to stop for a minute," Andrew said. *Tell Joe to rope somethin' with the Stone Rope.* "Joe, Pecos wants you to rope something with the Stone Rope."

"Sure thing," Joe said, stepping forward. He struggled to remove the rope from Peppermint, but he managed. Then he worked one end into a loop. He couldn't hold the entire rope in his left hand; it was so heavy he could only hold a couple gleaming coils. Then he tried to spin the loop over his head.

But he couldn't. No matter how hard Joe tried, the rope wouldn't budge, and Andrew's heart plummeted. Grandma had said Pecos could do it, but Andrew couldn't. Joe couldn't. This was not good. *Have Doyle and Charlie try.* "Doyle, Charlie," Andrew said, knowing it was pointless. "Would you try?"

Doyle stepped up first, but he couldn't spin it either. And neither could Charlie. The rope was simply too heavy.

We need a backup plan. Backup plan? *They can't use the rope, so you'll keep trainin'. If you'd just get out of the way, you could do it.* I CAN'T! *Not with that attitude, but we need somethin' else anyway; I've been thinkin' 'bout an army.*

Andrew snorted. Didn't you see what Septimis did to the men in that town? What good's an army gonna do? *Not an army of men, you idiot. An army of animals.* Animals? For real? *Get some more horses, then tell Charlie to go to Owl Haven.* Owl Haven? *Yep.* Andrew sighed. Trying to get information from these guys was like trying to pull teeth, not that he'd ever tried to pull a tooth, but he imagined it was really, really difficult.

When they arrived back at the village, Charlie bartered with a man and ended up with three horses and a saddle. Charlie removed his saddle from Jiminty, and Andrew started to put the new saddle on Dewmint. He still found it hard to believe he knew how to saddle a horse.

"Wait!" a voice called out, and Andrew turned to see Charlie's grandmother walking toward him, carrying a polished brown saddle in her hands. "I have been working on this saddle for many months. I did not know why. I saw it in a vision." She smiled at Andrew. "I see now it is for you."

She held it out to him, and Andrew sucked in a breath. He hadn't seen many saddles, five to be exact, but he could tell this one was a work of art. A large raven was stitched across the back of the saddle, and it looked so realistic Andrew wondered if it could take flight. Streams of grey, black, and white were interwoven along the sides of the seat until they met together in a burst of yellow underneath the saddle's horn.

"Thank you," Andrew said, grinning widely. "It's super cool! How much?"

She patted his hand. "It is for you."

Andrew watched her walk away with a frown. Shouldn't we give her something for it? *You heard her; it's yours.* Andrew shrugged, remembering what had happened the last time he'd ignored Pecos's advice. He saddled Dewmint with the new saddle and mounted.

Wow! This feels amazing! Your saddle feels like a rock compared to this thing! *Don't you talk 'bout my saddle that way. Ain't nothin' wrong with my saddle!* Come on! Do you feel this thing? *Yes, I feel it! And... you know... it is purty nice.* Told you so! *Whatever.* Hold on, did you just say "whatever"? *No!* You did! I heard you! *Did not; now shut up and ride!* Andrew threw back his head and laughed, then he nudged Dewmint and followed Charlie out of the village.

When the village was behind them, Andrew rode up to Charlie and said, "Pecos wants to go to Owl Haven."

"You sure?" Charlie asked doubtfully.

Andrew shrugged. "That's what he said. Is that bad?"

Charlie shook his head but didn't answer, and Andrew frowned. He was beginning to think he'd be better off just fighting Septimis.

They rode hard for several hours, switching horses often, but after midday, Charlie slowed their pace because of the intense heat. Joe rode beside Andrew, playing his harmonica. Andrew listened to the music, wondering what Owl Haven was, what Chuck and Ed were doing, why his dad never expected anything from him.

The more he thought about things, the more something bugged him. "Hey Joe," he said suddenly. "If you guys are ranchers like Pecos said, how come you need so many weapons? And why did you ride out to fight Septimis? Shouldn't you be taking care of cows or something?"

Joe's laughing eyes grew serious. "We've never just been ranchers. There're things in this world that defy explanation, like the snake or carnivorous dust devils, the spider clan or skinwalkers...there's a long list, and somebody has to fight them when they cause trouble, but not many people can. Not like Pecos. And then, of course, you got your run-of-the-mill problems like rustlers, outlaws, and no-good louses."

"I'm sorry…did you say carnivorous dust devils?" Joe nodded. Andrew was beginning to see he didn't know anything at all about the old west or whatever this was. "I'm only thirteen," he said softly. "How can I help anyone?"

"What does your age have to do with anything?"

"Everything! Back home I can't drive, can't have a job; I go to school and that's it."

"Different times, I guess," Joe said. "When I met Pecos, I was seventeen. Pecos was younger, but he taught me everything I know."

"What? That doesn't even make sense!"

Joe grinned widely. "Around here a boy's a man when he becomes a man. I became the man I wanted to be at eighteen. Who knows when Pecos became a man; maybe when he left his coyote pack."

"We've a man on our crew who's just ten," Joe continued. "And quite a few are between twelve and fifteen. And you're becoming a man at thirteen." Joe winked at him. "Welcome to the West."

"Wait, does that mean when you fought Pecos he was younger than you and he still won?"

"Yep," Joe said with a chuckle.

Andrew shook his head, trying to imagine working on a ranch when he was only ten years old. He didn't think he could handle being away from his mom, being a man, being responsible for himself. He thought about all the chores Grandpa Lester had had to do when he was young, like milking the cows and going to town for supplies. When he had told Andrew about the first time he'd taken the team to town on his own, Andrew hadn't believed him. "You were just nine," he'd said. "Nine year olds can't do stuff like that!"

Grandpa had snorted. "That's now; kids aren't allowed to grow up 'til it almost too late. Back then, we grew up young, and we were better for it." Maybe Grandpa had been right. Andrew couldn't help but think if Grandpa Lester were here instead of him, things would be going a bit more smoothly.

Chapter Ten

The heat of the day soon passed, and Charlie increased their pace again. Every time they stopped, one of the others helped Andrew move the Stone Rope from one horse to another. Andrew was dragging, barely awake, and terribly hungry by the time they stopped to eat. The sun was low in the sky, about to slip behind the horizon, and he fervently hoped they were done for the day.

"Are we stopping?" he asked Charlie.

"Nope."

"Course not," Andrew mumbled. "Can I have another cup of coffee then?"

Doyle grunted and filled Andrew's cup to the brim. Andrew sipped it quickly, trying not to burn his tongue, knowing they wouldn't wait for him to finish.

They rode into the night, and every time they stopped Andrew did jumping jacks in a desperate attempt to keep himself awake.

"What the hell you doin', boy?" Doyle growled.

"Trying to stay awake."

"You fallin' asleep in the saddle again?"

"I don't normally stay up this late, you know." *Sissy.*

"Kinda sissy, ain't you?" Doyle said, mounting his horse.

Andrew rolled his eyes. "Yep, that's me. Sissy boy." He mounted Dewmint and waited for Charlie to head out, then Andrew rode up beside him.

"How do you know where you're going?" he asked.

"Just do," Charlie replied.

"Why do you guys always say that? 'Just do,' 'Just is'; can't you ever answer a question?"

"Nope."

Andrew growled and pulled back on Dewmint's reins, slowing her until he was well behind Charlie. Tell me a story, Pecos, and make it a good one. *Did I tell you 'bout the time Doyle and I gave a whole village of skinwalkers a good talkin' to?* Skinwalkers? What're those? *Nasty creatures. Trade a bit of themselves to wear the skin of an animal.* Ugh. Why? *Power I guess. Anyway, Doyle and I were out on a round up and...*

Pecos went on and on, and Andrew listened raptly. Pecos's stories were so fantastic that the tall tales about him actually paled in comparison. But the way Pecos told his stories, the details he wove into them, Andrew could feel the truth in them, knew Pecos wasn't lying or embellishing. However fantastic or unreal it seemed, he was telling the truth.

Then there was this one time I went to find a basket woman. Basket woman? That doesn't sound like a big deal. *You wouldn't say that if one put you in her basket.* Um... *So anyway I had thought there was just one...*

That was a terrible story! Andrew snapped when Pecos had finished. *No it weren't. I won!* Yeah, but, yuck. I'm gonna have nightmares now. I mean...ugh. *Alright, how 'bout I tell you 'bout the time someone tried to steal Widow Maker?* Why would anyone try to steal a horse named Widow Maker? *Well...it weren't his name yet...*

By dawn, Andrew was slumped in his saddle, eyes barely open, but he sat up suddenly when he saw a structure rise out of the plains ahead of them. What the hell's that? *Owl Haven.* Owl Haven? That's where we're going? Why?!

Owl Haven was not a built structure; it was a living structure. Thousands, maybe millions of those creepy little cactuses had grown together, crawling up each other, growing taller and taller and wider. They had grown so tall in some places, they looked as if they could brush the clouds.

Andrew gulped. And what lives here? he asked, dreading the answer. *Owls, boy. It's right there in the name.* Of course it is. And why do we need owls? *To gather our army.* Oh. Great. So what now? *Why do I always gotta spell everythin' out for you?*

Andrew sighed and rode up beside Charlie. "So that's Owl Haven?" he asked, even though he already knew, part of him was hoping Charlie would say no and keep riding.

"Yep."

"You don't seem thrilled to see it."

"Don't care for owls myself."

"Oh. Fantastic."

Charlie stopped beside a solid cactus wall, and Andrew sat in his saddle, staring. *Get movin' boy!* Get moving where? *Inside.* Inside that? Are you crazy?! There's not even a way in. *Why do you always ask if*

I'm crazy? If one of us is crazy, it's you! Move your butt!

Andrew flinched as he slid slowly off Peppermint. They'd been riding so long, he could barely move his legs. *You're a disgrace! I've never been sore a day in my life.* There's a first time for everything, Andrew snapped, gasping as he tried to touch his toes. *When I get my hands on you...* Oh shut up. Stretching's good for you. *Says who?* Says everybody. The President even stretches. *What has the world come to?* Andrew laughed and stretched his arms high into the air.

The others had dismounted, and Andrew could see Joe's lips twitching with laughter but Doyle looked ready to break something. *Stop it! It's time to go.* Whatever; I was done anyway. How exactly are we doing this? *I'll show you. Tell the others to wait here.* What?! Why can't they come with us? *Better if you do this on your own.* Andrew frowned. Why do I always have to do it on my own? *Just do.*

Andrew sighed, but followed Pecos's directions to an entrance between two arching cactus plants. The opening was at least five feet off the ground, and Andrew stared into it in dismay. It opened into a high tunnel through the cactuses. Cactus spines covered the entire inside of the tunnel, and each spine was as long as one of Pecos's fingers.

And just how do you expect me to get through there? Pecos growled. *I expect you to take the knife out of my boot and use it to cut the spines off.* And then? *I expect you to crawl through the damn tunnel! Why you being so thick-headed?*

This is seriously your backup plan? Crawl through a cactus tunnel and talk to some owls? *You got a better plan, boy?* No. *Then get to it!* Andrew was so tired he wasn't sure he could even drag himself into the opening. Can I at least have some coffee first? *NO!* Fine. He should have read the library book his mom had brought him about leprechauns instead. They could have gotten a laugh out of it, and he was pretty sure leprechauns didn't think they were heroes.

Andrew pulled the knife from his boot and stared at it. Are you sure this isn't a sword? *What? Why would I have a sword in my boot?* Andrew laughed softly. He could feel the others behind him, watching him, so he clutched the knife and gingerly started to cut the spines off the cactuses. *You're gonna have to work faster than that, boy.* Andrew flinched as a spine stabbed into his knuckle and blood welled.

He paled as the blood dripped onto a cactus. Seeing it just reinforced that everything was real. They were going to fight a gigantic snake, and they were going to die. *We ain't gonna die.* Yes, we are. *Boy*... Why do we have to fight it anyway? Why you? *Who else is gonna do it?* I don't know, the President? The army? *Sure, I 'spect they might eventually get involved. After some more people get killed.* What? *Government don't usually concern themselves until there's a pretty big fuss. Even then though...* What? *Not sure what they could do. All they got is guns and explosives, and...well, you saw it.* Yes, he had seen it, so he knew exactly what Pecos meant.

Andrew closed his eyes, imagining his mom's laughing eyes and happy smile. He imagined her singing in the kitchen as she made him breakfast. He imagined her hugging him tightly.

Isn't there another way in? *Nope.* Andrew clutched the knife tightly, wishing Pecos would cut him some slack. He wasn't Pecos, he wasn't, and he didn't know why he had to act like he was. *Somebody's gotta do it, boy. I can't; so that leaves you.*

Andrew wiped the blood onto his pants and went back to work, faster this time. After he'd cleared a long section, he wiggled into the tunnel and crawled forward, inch by inch, cutting off the spines as he went.

He'd never worked so hard in his life, not even when Joe had tried to teach him to rope or when they'd ridden without stopping, and he didn't care for it. He wanted to quit and take a nap. He wanted to stop and roll into a ball with a warm blanket and never come out. He wanted a cup of hot cocoa. *Man up, boy!* Andrew sighed and kept cutting.

He cut because Pecos told him to, he cut because he really didn't have a choice. He may want to go home, but he couldn't. He may want to sleep, but Pecos would never let him. He may want to give up, but the truth was, deep down, he knew he had to do this. Knew he'd never be able to look himself in the eyes if he didn't. Knew he'd never get the sounds of those children screaming out of his head.

So he cut and cut and crawled and cut and crawled. By the time he'd made it through the twenty-foot tunnel, he was drenched in sweat and his hands and arms were covered in stinging cuts. Andrew ran a hand gently over his shoulder. It was wet, and when he looked at his hand it was smeared with blood.

He carefully put the knife back in his boot. *Wipe it off.* What? *Wipe the knife on your pants; otherwise it'll lose its sharpness.* Andrew removed the knife and wiped it carefully on his pants. His mom would faint if she saw him. What now? *Keep goin'. You ruined my favorite shirt, you know.* You're the one who told me to crawl through there. *I could've done it without gettin' cut.* Prove it. *Boy...*

The cactuses were still closed overhead, but they had opened into a large walkway, and Andrew was able to stand, although he still had to duck every now and then. He walked quickly along it, ducking and wiggling around spines as he went. Light filtered through the cactuses overhead creating a dim, greenish light. It made him feel like he was inside something's belly. Like a gigantic snake, he thought with a shudder.

It was oddly silent; the only sound a slight crunching under his boots. What's that crunching sound? he asked. *Probably best not to look.* Why? *Just 'cause.* Andrew frowned, bending and peering closely at the odd shaped white things covering the ground. He picked up a piece near his foot. Empty black eye holes peered back at him, and he yelped, jumping backwards and dropping the skull.

"These're bones!" he exclaimed. Everywhere he turned, bones covered the ground. He dug with his toe trying to feel the earth, but the bones were so thick he couldn't. What is this place? he asked in horror. *Owls gotta eat, you know.* Andrew cringed. But this...I mean...I don't like this. *You ain't an owl.*

The bones outside Grandfather Bear's cave had been terrifying, but these bones were sinister. They were laid out like a carpet, and Andrew hated it. He hated that he was stuck inside a gigantic cactus fort surrounded by bones. And I thought owls ate the bones. *I don't know, boy. I'm not a damn owl!*

Why're we doing this? Andrew asked, wishing he could turn and go the other way, dreading what he'd see at the end. *We need the owls to gather the other critters.* I take it these are talking owls? Andrew asked with a sigh. *Some.*

He started to walk forward again, wishing Doyle had come with him. Surely Doyle was scarier than a couple of talking owls. Pecos snorted. What? Andrew asked. *Nothin'.* You laughed. *Just don't get on Doyle's bad side.* Huh? *Nothin'.* The sun was high overhead now, and the heat was seeping through the cactuses. Sweat rolled down Andrew's arms making his cuts sting.

He walked carefully, trying very hard not to hear the crunch under his boots, humming to cover the sound. He closed his eyes as he crawled on his hands and knees through a tunnel. The bones cracked under his weight, and he wanted to gag, but he didn't.

The tunnel finally ended, and Andrew stepped slowly into a large clearing. There were several openings overhead, but the cactuses grew up, spreading in a dome over the entire clearing, closing it in and casting weird shadows on the ground. Andrew's mouth dropped open when he saw the dark brown and white owl resting on a lone cactus bunch in the middle, and he wished he was somewhere else, maybe even back with Grandfather Bear. The owl was bigger than Chuck and Ed's Great Dane, bigger than owls were meant to be. Andrew should have known, but he'd stupidly expected a normal-sized owl.

Its body didn't move, but its head swiveled around, and it stared at Andrew with glowing orange eyes. "Why have you come here, Not Pecos?" it asked in a raspy voice, stretching its sharp talons.

Andrew blinked in surprise, but recovered quickly. "Pecos is in here. With me. He wants to ask you to spread the word. We're building an army of animals to fight the father of snakes." *Get closer.* Seriously? *Seriously.* Andrew stepped two feet nearer; he'd intended to go further, but his feet simply refused to move.

The owl's brilliant orange eyes peered into Andrew's. Its beak was wide and long and curved, and Andrew tried to ignore the red that coated its claws and beak and splattered across its feathers, but he couldn't. And in spite of his efforts to pretend otherwise, he knew exactly what it was.

"Septimis does not harm us," the owl said, eyes closing and opening unhurriedly.

"Oh…" Andrew said, thinking it out. As far as he knew Septimis was only killing people, the ones who killed his children and turned them into clothing. So, the owl was right. Septimis wasn't harming them.

"Why would the animals join you in this fight?" the owl continued. "It seems to me the earth would benefit from a few less humans. Especially the infectious white man."

Andrew grimaced. He was trapped inside a gigantic cactus fortress with an owl who hated humans, especially white humans, which both he and Pecos happened to be. Orange globes blinked all around him, hundreds and hundreds of them, staring right at him. Scratch that. He was trapped inside a cactus fortress with hundreds of owls who hated him.

Pecos? *What?* This was your plan. *I'm thinkin', boy.* Think faster! "Seems like when Septimis runs out of people to eat, he might turn to animals," Andrew said, trying to act casual. "Don't snakes eat birds?"

"Or maybe," the owl replied with a narrow-eyed glare, "when his revenge is complete, he will return to his sleep, full and content."

"Or that," Andrew conceded. Owls were crawling out of the cactuses now, surrounding him, standing all around him, eyes blinking, beaks clicking, talons flexing. Andrew was starting to see why Charlie didn't like owls. He swallowed. PECOS!

"But you will not be there to see it," the owl remarked carelessly. The owls moved closer. "Because you are going to be a very tasty snack."

What?! Why does everything wanna eat me? Andrew asked as he reached for his gun, knowing it was useless against so many owls, wishing the others were with him, wishing he'd had time to train more. *Get ready to run, boy!*

An owl swooped across the clearing towards Andrew, and Andrew jumped to the side, moving faster than he knew he could, grabbing the owl as it flew past and shoving it into a cactus behind him. He yelped in pain when the spines ran through the owl straight into his hand.

He ripped his hand free and spun around, drawing his gun and firing all six shots directly into the midsection of the owl leader. Blood spurted from its chest as Andrew's bullets hit true. *Really wish you hadn't done that, boy. RUN!*

Andrew didn't pause to ask why, just jumped back into the tunnel, scrambling through it as fast as he could, hearing the squawks and hoots of the angry owls behind him. He tumbled out the other end, landing hard on his backside in the dirt.

"RIDE!" he screamed, running towards the horses. But it was too late. The owls had already gathered in the air above him, hooting angrily. The others drew their guns and started firing as the owls dived towards Andrew, claws outstretched.

Andrew heard their gunshots and scrambled to his feet, fumbling to pull his gun, raising it, trying to aim, and firing; but nothing happened. He hadn't reloaded. He dropped the gun and grabbed another one. The owls were so close now he could see their narrowed eyes. He fired madly into the mass of them, then wrapped his arms around his head just as the owls were upon him, but their claws never touched him. Instead they suddenly turned and returned to the cactus fortress.

Within seconds it was so quiet, Andrew wouldn't have believed it had even happened, except for the dead owls scattered around him.

"What happened?" Doyle snapped.

"Pecos didn't have a plan!" Andrew yelled. *I had a plan; just didn't go as I planned.* Andrew rolled his eyes. "They don't care about the snake. They were gonna eat me!"

An owl twitched near Doyle, and Doyle shot it. The bullet slammed into it, snapping it into the ground. "Can we get out of here?" Andrew asked with a shudder.

"Where we goin'?" Charlie asked.

"I don't know, damn it!" Pecos? Where're we going? *Towards the snake.* What?! *We'll go slow. I've still got a plan.* I don't wanna hear any more of your plans. Your plans get me eaten! *Quit your whinin'; you didn't get eaten.* Andrew frowned, figuring the chances he'd get eaten by the father of all snakes were pretty high.

"Pecos says to head towards the snake." *We'll stop early, and you can train.* Great. "We'll stop early so I can train," Andrew added, wishing Pecos had said they would stop early so he could sleep. He needed a nap. And a new heart. This one was worn out from hammering so hard all the time. *Boy...you're a disgrace.* Really? A disgrace? I think I did pretty good considering, Andrew snapped.

"Let's ride," Charlie said.

Andrew pulled himself into his saddle and followed Charlie, glad Charlie set a fast pace. He wanted to get far away from Owl Haven, as far as possible.

Chapter Eleven

So what's your plan now? Andrew asked Pecos as they galloped over the prairie. *Hasn't changed. You train; gather an army.* How could it not have changed?! And how're we gonna gather an army? That owl was right, you know. Why would the animals help us? Septimis isn't hurting them. *I'll figure it out.*

When Charlie slowed the pace, Andrew rode up beside him. "So how come not all animals talk?" Andrew asked.

"The elders say at the dawn of life all animals could."

"So what happened?"

"No one knows. The old ones talk. Some of the young talk. But most animals don't."

"It's really weird when they do," Andrew said cringing. "Like the owl, his beak moved and words came out, but it just didn't look right. And how come they speak English anyway? That just seems…wrong."

"I don't think they do speak English."

"Whadda you mean? I can understand them, so they must be speaking English."

"I think…" Charlie paused, brow furrowed. "I think they speak the original tongue."

"Original tongue?"

"The first language all man spoke."

"Then how come I can understand them?"

"Because each of us, deep down, know the original tongue and understand it."

Andrew stared at Charlie in disbelief. "That's crazy! All of this is crazy. If I hadn't bled so much already I'd still be convinced you were knife-me, Doyle was angry-me, and Joe was mustached-me. And all of this was a crazy dream inside my head."

"Knife-me?"

"Yeah, like you're really just a version of me because I made all this up. And that's how you knew I wasn't Pecos but was instead me. Even though Pecos is me." *You got heat sickness, boy?*

Charlie chuckled softly. "So do you?"

"Do I what?"

"Believe it's a dream?"

Andrew breathed deeply, feeling the air fill his lungs, feeling the heat on his neck, feeling the incredible ache inside all his muscles and bones, feeling the terror thrumming in the back of his head, waiting to be set loose. "No," he said softly. "It's real. I don't understand how, but it is."

"So what happened at Owl Haven?" Charlie asked.

"They weren't interested in helping," Andrew replied, glad for the change in subject. "They attacked, so I shot the big owl and crawled out through the tunnel."

Charlie's face blanked. "You killed the old one?"

"What? You mean the big owl? I don't know. I shot it like six times. It bled, but I didn't stick around."

"Why'd you shoot 'im?"

"Don't they always say to go for the leader?"

"Not when the leader's an old one."

"What does that even mean, old one?"

"The old ones are old, perhaps not the first, but very, very, very old. The second, third, who knows. Grandfather Bear is an old one. If you killed the old one…"

"What?" Andrew asked, dreading the answer.

"The owls'll hunt you. Forever."

"Hunt me? They were gonna eat me!"

"You killed one of their fathers."

Well crap. It just got worse and worse. Why didn't you tell me? Andrew snapped at Pecos. *Too late.* Figures. I'm sorry. *What for?* The owls. Didn't you hear Charlie? *Ain't nothin' huntin' me, boy.* But…but…I'm in your body. YOU shot the owl. *Nope. You did.* What're you saying? *I'm sayin' the owls'll be huntin' YOU, not me.* Andrew sighed. Maybe today was the worst day ever. If he was ordering them, which he wasn't.

They rode for hours without speaking. Even Pecos didn't speak, and Andrew hoped he was busy thinking of a new plan, a plan that might actually work. Andrew tried to watch the landscape and feel the rhythm of his horses, but his mind kept slipping back to the town. He kept watching those men die, watching them be crushed by those huge green scales and eaten by those gigantic jaws. And he kept imaging it was him. He didn't know what Pecos was thinking. Andrew couldn't fight Septimis and win. It wasn't possible. He was just a boy.

He felt like his entire world had crumbled to pieces around him. Everything he'd understood and thought to be true was being called into question. Time travel, magic, talking animals, a snake bigger than a train, called the father of all snakes because he was literally the father of all snakes.

This stuff didn't exist, or it shouldn't exist, or it did exist and everyone had been lying to him his entire life. Did anyone know? Did his mom know? The President? Someone had to know. But even though Andrew's head was spinning like a top and he couldn't get a grip on anything, Pecos still thought he could do this, still thought Andrew could be him. It'd be laughable if it wasn't so terrifying.

When the sun hung low in the sky, they finally stopped just inside a pine forest. Andrew slipped from his horse, pulled the Stone Rope from the extra saddle, and stripped the saddles from both his horses. "Hey, Charlie," he said, rubbing the horses down. "Do these new horses have names?"

"Nope," Charlie said.

"Sweet. I'll name them."

"Wouldn't bother," Doyle said gruffly.

"Why not?" Andrew asked, but Doyle didn't answer. Andrew shrugged and studied the horses. One was a lighter buckskin color than Peppermint, one was black with white socks, and one was white with black specks. Andrew rubbed the buckskin's nose. "I'll call you Babe." *What kinda name's that?* It's just as good as Jiminty. *Really not.* My horses; my names; shut up. He rubbed the black one's head. "You'll be Mays, and you'll be Jeter." *Quit messin' around, boy,* Pecos humphed. *You got work to do.* Don't get your panties in a twist. *My what?!* Your panties, underwear, oh never mind.

Andrew scanned the trees for owls. He absolutely hated the idea of them hunting him. They were night creatures, and he'd never been fond of the dark. It was just so...unknown. He shuddered remembering their long talons and blood covered beaks.

"Follow me," Charlie said when Andrew was done with his horses. Charlie walked deeper into the woods, and after a bit, he stopped and handed Andrew a humongous knife.

"Whoa!" Andrew said in surprise, taking the knife with a shaking hand. "Are you sure this knife's legal? It's even bigger than Pecos's. It's like two feet long!"

Charlie looked confused. "Ain't no such thing as an outlawed knife."

"Maybe not where you're from."

Charlie frowned. "You have outlawed knives?"

"Yeah, a lot of stuff's illegal. You can't just walk around with guns and stuff. And in some towns, you can't even carry a knife if the blade's over two inches." *No wonder you're such a sissy.*

"Two inches?" Charlie asked in surprise. "What good's that?"

"I don't know." Andrew turned the knife over in his hand. The blade was bright and shiny, and it looked very, very sharp. He resisted the urge to run his finger down the blade to see how sharp it was and handed it back to Charlie. "How's it work, anyway?"

"It doesn't. You do," Charlie replied with a slight grin. "We'll work on throwin'. Hand to hand is best avoided." He pointed at a tree about twenty feet away. "That's our target. I'll show you a couple ways to throw, and we'll see what you do best. For an overhand throw, hold the knife like this."

Charlie pulled back his arm, then whipped it forward, and the knife went sailing through the air. It landed with a heavy thunk in the very middle of the tree trunk. Before Andrew could even say "wow", Charlie had thrown six more knives, which landed in a perfect circle around the first.

"Dude!" Andrew exclaimed. "That was amazing! You're so fast!"

Charlie grinned; then he retrieved the knives and handed one to Andrew. "You try now."

"No way I'll be able to do that."

Charlie shrugged. "Today's for learnin'."

Andrew looked at the knife. It felt heavy and awkward in his hand. "Just throw it?" he asked doubtfully.

"Yep."

Andrew drew his hand back the way Charlie had and threw the knife. It flew wobbly through the air and landed several feet away. *Did you even try, boy? I sure as hell hope not.* It was just my first throw, Andrew thought, face flushing. He picked up the knife and tried again, throwing harder this time.

"Yes! That's gotta be at least twelve feet!" He did a little dance. *You've got all the strength of my body,* Pecos ground out; *and the most you can throw is twelve measly feet? I can throw a knife a quarter of a mile.* No one can do that, Andrew snorted. *I can!* Prove it. *Boy, how can I do that with you foolin' 'round with my body and makin' me look like some kinda fool?* Exactly! *What's that supposed to mean?* You say all this stuff 'bout how you can do this and you can do that, but you can't prove it, so shut the hell up!

Andrew closed his eyes, trying to physically push Pecos away, but he couldn't. No matter how hard he pushed he could still hear Pecos ranting and raving. He opened his eyes with a sigh and focused on the knife in his hand.

Charlie moved them closer to the tree, and Andrew threw the knife again. This time the handle hit the middle of the tree, and the knife bounced to the ground.

"You got good aim," Charlie said. "Let's try underhand." Charlie showed Andrew how to hold the knife underhanded and when to release it. When Charlie threw the knife, it flew straight into the tree without spinning once. "Handy throw if you're close."

Andrew held the knife carefully and threw it underhand. It slipped, hit a tree on Andrew's far left, and plopped to the ground. Andrew grimaced. *I can't watch.* Then don't! Andrew snapped. He tried the underhand throw again; this time it sailed off to his right and into a bush.

"Let's stick with overhand," Charlie said. He moved Andrew's arm and showed him how to carry the arc and when to release the knife. Andrew threw. The knife bounced off the tree. "You ain't gettin' quite enough spin. Keep tryin'; it's just like a horse. Once you find the rhythm, it'll be easy."

Andrew threw and threw and threw. For every one time he managed to stick the knife into the tree, it bounced fifteen times. His arm was starting to ache, but Charlie just kept adjusting and telling him to try again. Every time Andrew missed it just reminded him why he couldn't do this. He wasn't good at anything; and he certainly wouldn't be good at fighting an evil monster snake.

"Can I take a break?" Andrew finally asked. He was exhausted. He couldn't remember the last time he'd slept, and he was apparently an abysmal failure. He could barely ride, he couldn't rope, he couldn't throw a knife. The only thing he could do was shoot a gun, and that was probably only because he'd played so many video games.

"Ten more."

Andrew frowned, wishing he were home, throwing the winning pitch. Pitching didn't save anyone's life, but at least he was good at it. He threw the knife fast and hard, and it stuck with a boing. He walked forward, ripped it out angrily, and threw it again. It stuck again. And again and again.

Andrew stopped. He had stuck the knife four times in a row, and he hadn't even been trying. What was he doing differently? He tried to remember how he'd been throwing it. He hadn't been paying attention, he'd stopped trying to control the knife, and he'd been throwing it like he pitched a ball. Maybe that was the trick. He threw it again, mimicking his pitching motion. It stuck!

"I'm doing it! Did you see that, Charlie? I stuck it five times!"

Charlie grinned at him. "It ain't spinnin', so you don't have to worry 'bout adjustin' for distance."

Andrew threw six more times, and each time it stuck fast in the wood. He finally handed the knife back to Charlie with a wide grin. "That was awesome! It's not really all that different from pitching."

"Pitchin'?"

"Baseball. It's a game I play back home. I pitch a ball to the batters, and they try to hit it. When can I try that thing?" Andrew asked, pointing to the tomahawk fastened to Charlie's side.

Charlie grinned. "Many, many, many, many moons from now. Many."

"Huh. What about the bow?"

"Patience. Knife first."

Andrew grunted. Did you see how good I did, Pecos? *Sure. Now if only that onery ol' snake will come right up to you and hold still while you throw a knife at it.* Andrew rolled his eyes. It was annoying that Pecos was so good at everything. Isn't there something you have to work at? *No.* Whatever.

Andrew plopped down next to the campfire, exhausted and ready to sleep. But the smell of burning biscuits made his stomach growl. He waited sadly for Doyle to fill his plate, happy to take the cup of coffee to wash everything down. He wouldn't admit it, not to Doyle anyway, but he was actually starting to like coffee. Not the biscuits though. If only his mom were here. She knew how to make biscuits; Doyle didn't seem to have ever learned.

He took a bite of biscuit and a drink of coffee, but frowned as he swallowed. "What's this?" he asked.

"What's what?" asked Joe.

"This!" Andrew said, holding up his coffee cup.

"Coffee. You hit your head on something?"

Andrew sniffed the cup. It smelled like coffee, but it wasn't black enough, and it didn't taste right. "This isn't coffee, is it? It's…I dunno…weak."

"I made it," Charlie said.

"Really? Why?"

"Sometimes Charlie likes to make the coffee, boy," Doyle said with a chuckle. "Says it tastes better when he does it."

"Huh. I see." It didn't taste better. It was weak, and Andrew didn't like it nearly as much, but he didn't want to hurt Charlie's feelings, so he drank it anyway.

Andrew had just polished off his plate when a "tsk, tsk" sounded beside him. He jerked sideways, but forced himself to still when he saw it was the Grey Shaman. "Can't you just walk into camp?" Andrew demanded. "Do you have to pop?"

"It's part of my charm," the Grey Shaman said, smiling widely. "Waging war against the old ones? Bold."

"I didn't know, damn it! How was I supposed to know?"

"Just do," Charlie said from across the fire.

"Just do, just do," Andrew mocked. "I've never even heard of an old one until today! I doubt there even are old ones in my time."

"Perhaps not. What now?" the Grey Shaman asked.

"I don't know. Pecos says I train and we build an army of animals. But that owl was right. Why would the animals help us? Men hunt and kill them. Why would they care if Septimis takes out a thousand or even a million?"

The Grey Shaman pulled a tin cup from his bag and filled it with coffee. He took a careful sip. "Nicely done, Charlie," he said. Then he gazed at the fire thoughtfully before saying, "I suppose you must give them a reason to join. A reason...or a common enemy." And then, just like before, he was gone.

Andrew shuddered. "That is so creepy! I wish he wouldn't do that."

"Just part of his charm," Joe drawled, and then for some reason they were laughing. They laughed just like they did everything else, big; and before long Andrew was only laughing because they were laughing. When they finally stopped, he had to wipe tears from his eyes.

Joe pulled out his harmonica and began playing a slow melody, and Andrew's eyes slipped closed. He started to fall sideways, but jerked awake. *Go to sleep, boy,* Pecos said softly. Andrew nodded, tucking his saddle blanket under his head and pulling his hat over his eyes. A pang of intense homesickness gripped him. He missed his mom. He missed her laugh and her happy chatter. He sighed, pushing thoughts of her aside, and drifted off to sleep.

He dreamed the dark was eating the entire land, devouring everything in its path, turning everything into death. When it was done the whole world was black. And then an owl flew out of the blackness and pecked out Andrew's eyes.

Something grabbed him, and Andrew punched out wildly, kicking his legs and growling. "Wake up, boy!" a voice shouted, and Andrew paused, forcing his eyes open, sagging with relief when he recognized Doyle. "Time to go," Doyle snapped. Andrew nodded and rolled to his feet.

For a moment he stood still, breathing, reminding himself it had only been a dream. A horrible dream, a nightmare, but a dream none-the-less. The earth wasn't black, and he still had his eyes. He rubbed a shaking hand over his face, surprised to feel rough, scratchy whiskers. He missed his face and hands. He missed his body. Pecos's body was fine for Pecos, but he could have it. Andrew wanted his own body back.

He wondered if it was the dark that had brought him. Maybe the dark wanted to kill Pecos, and what better way to do it than by dropping an idiot, know-nothing kid inside his body?

Andrew took the coffee cup Doyle held out to him and took a deep sip. The sun wasn't even close to rising. If he was going to make it through another day, he was going to need two cups, maybe even three.

Chapter Twelve

They rode silently through the rest of the night and into the dawn. For a while Andrew closed his eyes and focused on Pecos's strength, trying desperately to touch it. He could see it, he could feel the heat of it, but no matter what, whenever he reached for it, it ran away and he was left with nothing.

When sleep began to lull him under, he asked Pecos to tell him another story. *You tell me a story, boy.* What? I don't think so. *Why not?* Um…because my life isn't exciting. In fact, it's pretty dull. If I told you a story, we'd both fall asleep.

What 'bout your leg? What about it? *Broken?* Oh, well, that wasn't really exciting. It was dumb. That's what it was. *Why's that?* Andrew sighed. The thing is, I'm not supposed to climb trees. *What?!* My mom…she worries. If I had any siblings maybe she wouldn't worry so much, but I don't, so. Anyway. *Your leg?* Right.

Well, I picked the biggest tree in the park, and I climbed it. It was awesome. I mean, I'd never been so high outside of a building. But then… *Yeah?* It sounds kinda stupid now, but there was this cat. I swear this cat was half puma. Huge, mangy, grey thing. And just all of the sudden, when I was almost to the top, it jumped down at me, claws out, teeth bared, hissing, foaming at the mouth. Andrew was exaggerating just a little, but he didn't want Pecos to think he was anymore of a weenie than he already did.

And...well...I let go. *You let go?* Yep. I let go, fell, and broke my leg in three places. First thing my mom says after she makes sure I'm alright is "And this is why I told you to never climb trees!" Pecos laughed, and Andrew grinned. Anyway, so that's the story, and the most exciting thing that's ever happened to me. So, you gonna tell me a story or am I gonna fall asleep in the saddle again? Pecos muttered something, but after a moment he said, *Did I tell you 'bout the time I met a man who could make it rain?*

Pecos told story after story, and Andrew listened intently, wishing his life was even a tiny bit as exciting as Pecos's was. *I gotta think now, boy. You keep yourself awake,* Pecos said just before dawn. Andrew laughed. Like he could fall asleep after that last story. He shuddered and watched the shadows deepen, wondering if there was anything hiding in them.

As day began to break, they rode through a patch of ground covered in short, scrubby, strong-smelling plants. Andrew was focusing on breathing in time with Dewmint's rhythm, and he inhaled deeply and sneezed. "What's this crap?" he asked Joe between sneezes.

"Sage brush."

"It stinks!" Andrew sneezed again. Hey, Pecos, you got a Kleenex? *A what?* A Kleenex, you know, to blow your nose on. *Hanky's in my pocket.* Andrew reached into his pocket and pulled out a red square of cloth. And what exactly do you expect me to do with this?

Blow your nose in it. Then what? *Put it back in your pocket.* Uh....seriously?! Have you used this thing before? *Course I've used it! That's what a hanky's for, boy.* Andrew stared at the hanky. His nose was running, but there was no way he was blowing his nose into a hanky Pecos had already used.

He shoved it gingerly back into his pocket and wiped his nose on his sleeve. *Did you just wipe your nose on my sleeve?* Duh. *That's a filthy thing to do; don't you ever do it again!* Not any filthier than reusing a hanky five million times. *Boy, I'm warnin' you.* Look Pecos, I'll use the john because I have to, but I don't have to use your damn hanky! That's disgusting! *I'm gonna let Doyle skin you,* Pecos snarled. How you gonna tell him to do it? 'Cause I'm sure as hell not telling him.

We've got bigger problems anyway, Andrew thought angrily. Do you have a plan yet? *Still thinkin'.* You don't have a plan, do you? What about a common enemy? What's the dark thing or whatever it was that whispered in Septimis's ear? *Don't know.* Well maybe we should find out. *Don't got time, boy. Snake's probably already destroyed a dozen or more towns, dependin' on how fast he's movin'. We've gotta stop him. You gotta figure out how to use my strength.*

Andrew didn't hear what else Pecos said. All he could hear were the screams, all he could feel was the fear, all he could see were more and more people being crushed to death, eaten, and slaughtered by Septimis. And it was his fault. His fault because he was here and

Pecos wasn't. And for a moment he couldn't breathe, but then he forced air into his lungs.

He closed his eyes, dreaming of home, dreaming of his stupid neon stars, dreaming of his broken leg, trying to make it real, trying to go there. Trying to get out of the way so Pecos could win. But when he opened his eyes, they were still Pecos's.

He had to be Pecos. He had to. After all, what good was an animal army against a gigantic snake that couldn't be hurt by bullets or arrows? He couldn't figure out why Pecos kept insisting they needed an army.

I'll try, Andrew thought. *You don't try, boy! You do!* I don't know how! I can see your power, but I can't touch it, can't use it. I'll try. That's the best I can do. *Do you TRY to drink a cup of coffee? No! You drink it!* Pecos snapped. But what if it's super hot? You might try it, then drink it later, you know? *Boy...you are the most confoundin', irritatin', idiotic....* Pecos went on and on, but Andrew ignored him, trying to feel the power inside him, trying to touch it, trying to make it his own.

It was fully light now, and Joe dropped back to ride beside Andrew. "It always amazes me," Joe said softly, looking around them.

"What?"

"The light, the day, everything." Joe grinned widely. "When I was young I don't think I saw a single sunrise or sunset; now I see them almost every single day."

"You weren't always a cowboy?" Andrew asked in surprise.

"Nope."

"What'd you do before?"

"Let's practice your roping while we ride," Joe said, ignoring Andrew's question.

Andrew groaned. "Do we have to? Can't I just walk up and grab things by the horns or something?"

Joe chuckled loudly. "You could try, but that's not going to work with Septimis."

"What about if I just hold the rope out, and he slithers into it?"

"I don't think so," Joe said with a grin.

"Humph. Shouldn't we wait until we stop?" *Quit your whinin', boy!*

"Nope. Most times you aren't going to be standing still, so this is better anyway."

Andrew rolled his eyes. Apparently Joe had an answer for everything; except for the questions he didn't want to answer.

It didn't take Andrew long to realize he was just as bad at roping from horseback as he was on the ground. Every time he missed, Pecos groaned. And every time he missed backwards, Joe groaned. It was embarrassing. Andrew hadn't been so embarrassed since first grade when his teacher had asked him to read a sentence aloud and he couldn't and all the other kids had laughed at him.

He wanted to quit after his first try. He wanted to burn the rope so he never had to see it again. He wished Pecos were in control so he could throw the rope somewhere far away like Canada. But he kept trying. He kept trying because he knew thousands of people were going to die if he didn't figure out how to rope. And use Pecos's strength. And figure out a way to use Pecos's strength to rope Septimis. He should have drunk more coffee.

He tried to rope cactuses, he tried to rope sage brush, he tried to rope scraggly trees, he tried to rope dead wood. But the only thing he ever managed to rope was Doyle, and that was by accident. Doyle gave him such a glare Andrew's insides turned cold.

Well, if he didn't like you before... I get it, Pecos. Doyle doesn't like me. And who cares who Doyle likes anyway? I don't know Doyle. He could be some kinda crazy person who...who... collects hankies! Pecos started laughing, and he didn't stop for a long time. You know it's kinda annoying having you laugh inside my head, Andrew thought irritably when Pecos finally quit. *It's my head, you idiot!*

After a while Andrew's shoulder hurt so badly he couldn't spin the rope even one more time, so he pulled it in and wrapped it up, hooking it to the side of his saddle. "Maybe we could work on something else?" he asked Joe hopefully.

"Sure. How about you practice shooting? Wouldn't do for you to lose any of Pecos's knives."

Andrew laughed hollowly. Wouldn't do indeed. He didn't want to talk to Doyle, but he figured he had to. They were kind of like teachers. Charlie was the horse and knife teacher, Joe was the rope teacher, and Doyle was the gun teacher. If only one of them could teach him how to actually BE Pecos.

Andrew nudged Dewmint softly and rode up next to Doyle. "Hi…um…Joe thought maybe I should work on shooting some."

"Why?" Doyle grunted.

"So I...um...get better?"

"I'd be crazy to let you shoot from horseback. You're plum dangerous, boy. You can't rope nothin', but you somehow managed to rope me."

Andrew frowned. He could see Doyle's point. "Well…I am a little better at shooting than roping."

"Nope," Doyle growled. "Your guns loaded?"

"No." Andrew hadn't bothered to reload after Owl Haven. He didn't particularly like the idea of riding around with loaded guns. What if one of them went off? *No use even carrin' 'em if you ain't gonna load 'em.* I know, but what if I shoot myself…I mean YOU, in the foot? *Disgrace.* Andrew sighed. He should just stop. He should ride off into the hills somewhere and take a nap. He should fall off Dewmint, hit his head, and see if he woke up in his own body.

"Draw and aim," Doyle said. "Like this." He pulled one of his guns and aimed at a tree. Then he put it away. "Over and over and over," he snarled.

"Fine," Andrew said, rolling his eyes. He double checked his gun to make sure it was empty, then he drew and aimed at a tree limb. He put it back and drew again. His arm got so tired, he switched hands. Left handed felt really weird, but he did it anyway. Pecos could probably shoot with his feet; the least Andrew could do was learn to use both hands.

By the time they quit riding, Andrew was exhausted. He slid off Jiminty, unsaddled the horses, rubbed them down, and plopped down on the ground beside them. He'd just started to drown in the blood of all the people Septimis had slaughtered when Charlie kicked his boot, waking him up.

"What?!" Andrew snapped. "Haven't I worked hard enough today? Can't I even take a nap? What is wrong with you guys?"

"Got work to do," Charlie said with a slight grin.

"This violates child labor laws," Andrew growled, pushing himself to his feet. *You're such a sissy it pains me.* I don't care if it does! I'm tired. I've been working hard, and all I get is a kick to the boot. *Sissy,* Pecos hissed. Damn it, Pecos! I'm trying! Call me sissy again, and I'll shoot your damn pinky toe off! *You wouldn't dare.* Try me!

Andrew ground his teeth and followed Charlie to a fallen tree right outside of camp. "Joe's right," Charlie said matter-of-factly. "Most of the time either you or what you're aimin' at'll be in motion. Or both. Standin' still don't make much sense. Throw a few times from here, then we'll try somethin' else."

Andrew wanted to sit down and cry, but he nodded and pulled his knife, throwing it like he pitched a ball. It stuck. Six times he threw, and six times the knife stuck, mostly right on target.

"Good; now try this," Charlie said. He ducked behind a tree, leaned out, threw his knife, and quickly hid again before his knife even buried into the tree.

"That is so cool," Andrew breathed. Charlie looked just like a super-awesome action hero. Andrew hid behind the tree and tried to mimic Charlie's actions. He pitched the knife and ducked back behind the tree. "Did I hit it?" he asked.

Charlie chuckled softly. "You hit somethin'."

"It wasn't Doyle, was it?" Andrew gasped.

"No," Charlie laughed.

Andrew looked around the tree. He didn't see his knife anywhere. "What did I hit then?"

"Dirt. Somewhere over there." Charlie pointed to the left of the tree.

At least it wasn't Doyle, Andrew thought with a sigh as he went to find his knife. After five minutes of searching he finally found it under a pile of pine needles.

He tried again and again and again. He only hit the tree once before Charlie finally let him quit. "So now I'm only good at stationary shooting and knife throwing, and I'm practically useless at everything else," Andrew complained as they walked back to camp.

"Not too bad on a horse."

"Thanks Charlie. That was a glowing compliment. Appreciate it."

Andrew didn't talk while he ate his dried meat and burnt biscuits, and he drank his coffee in sullen silence. He was a failure. An abysmal failure. The others ignored him, and when Joe pulled out his harmonica, Andrew shoved his head under his saddle blanket and tried to go to sleep.

He was tired and his body ached, but he couldn't fall asleep. He missed home. He missed his mom. He missed her cheerful voice in the morning, her laughter, the way she said his name. He hadn't heard his name in days. How many days had he been here? He couldn't even remember.

He hoped he wasn't dead. He hoped he got to go home someday. He didn't want his mom always wondering what had happened to him. If he did make it home, he'd never climb a tree ever again and he'd punch Chuck in the junk for taunting him into it. Joe's music filtered through the blanket, a solid reminder that Andrew wasn't home, but here, wherever here was, and he fell asleep wondering why he'd been the one chosen. Why not Chuck or Ed? Or anyone else?

He was so cold his body shook violently. He couldn't feel his hands or feet. He couldn't feel his face. And it was dark. So dark. Oppressively dark, like he imagined the inside of a coffin must be. Was he inside a coffin? Was he dead? He reached for the lid, panic making him sick, but there was nothing there.

He shuffled forward, but he couldn't see a thing, didn't know where he was. Could this be death? This blackness? He heard a soft noise, a chanting. At first he couldn't understand it, didn't know the words, but suddenly he did.

"Death, death, blood. Bright, bright blood. Feed me. Feed meeeee!"

Andrew's heart pounded in terror, but he couldn't move. The voice came closer, closer, and finally Andrew's legs moved, and he ran. He ran through the dark; he ran through the dark and out into the light. But the light was wrong. It was orange, and it blinked like an eye.

He was surrounded by owls. Thousands of them. They were on top of him, and they were pecking at him, ripping at him, stripping the flesh from his bones. He woke screaming, arms flailing. His eyes focused, and he felt acute relief when he saw the fire glowing beside him.

"Guess it's time to ride then," Joe drawled from across the fire.

Andrew was glad it was still dark, because his cheeks flamed when Joe spoke. Couldn't he even keep from embarrassing himself in his sleep? Only babies wake up screaming, he thought irritably as he pushed himself to his feet. He couldn't have been asleep for more than a couple hours, and he was so sick of being tired. Couldn't he have just one good night's sleep? Even four or five hours would do, as long as they were free of the nightmares that had been plaguing him.

Are these your dreams? he asked Pecos as he mechanically saddled Jiminty, too tired to even question what he was doing. *Nope. All yours, boy.* Can you see them? *Nope.* Where're you then? *Right here. Thinkin'.* Don't you sleep? Pecos didn't answer, and Andrew sighed. It seemed like Pecos and the others didn't answer a lot of questions. That must be in the cowboy rulebook.

Chapter Thirteen

They rode through the night without incident, stopping briefly at first light to eat and drink a cup of coffee. Andrew was beginning to crave that morning, afternoon, evening, and night cup of tar, and it scared him. Did he want the coffee or did Pecos want the coffee? Where did he end and Pecos begin?

He tried not to think about it, tried not to think about if he'd ever be himself again. Instead he spent the morning not roping with Joe, ignoring Pecos's comments, suggestions, orders, and insults. Then he spent the afternoon not shooting things. All in all, it was a very long day, and by late afternoon, he was sick of it.

He rode up by Charlie and asked irritably, "So what're we doing anyway?"

"Ridin' back to the snake."

"Why?"

Charlie cast him a long look. "To kill 'im."

Andrew snorted. "We know we can't. We couldn't raise an army; I can't use Pecos's strength; no one but Pecos can use that damn rope! What's the point?!"

"To try."

"That's stupid!" Andrew snapped. *Boy, ain't nothin' stupid 'bout fightin' for what's right.* Shut up Pecos! It's not like you have a plan! You don't know how to raise an army, and you can't teach me how to be you! We're gonna die! *Listen, boy...* No you listen! I'm so sick of you telling me what to do and how to act, calling me names, calling me "boy", calling me "sissy" and "idiot"! Sick of it! Stop telling me what to do!

Boy... "I SAID SHUT UP, PECOS!!!" Andrew yelled, slapping his heels into Dewmint's side. Dewmint reared and took off at a run, dashing over the open plain, running past cactuses and rocks, running towards the horizon, running towards silence. All Andrew wanted was some silence. He didn't want to hear Pecos in his head or the others correcting his every move. He didn't want to hear Doyle growl or snarl or Joe chuckle. He just wanted to be alone.

And so he rode. He rode and rode, and when his extra horses started to drag, he set them loose and kept riding. He was so angry, so tired, so sick of looking stupid and inept. He just wanted to go home. Home; where he was nothing, and no one expected anything from him.

Boy... I don't wanna hear it Pecos! I just need a minute. Please! *Now just ain't the right time.* Damn it! I don't give a rat's ass about that stupid snake! Let it eat the entire world for all I care!

Look around, boy. Andrew finally looked past his hands, past Dewmint's streaming mane, past the wateriness of his eyes. He looked up and saw nothing. Nothing but dust.

He pulled back on Dewmint's reins, but she jerked her head, reared, and kept running. Um...what's going on? *Dust devils. Whole bunch of 'em from the looks of it. And I hear at least one wind witch.* Wind witch? What the hell's a wind witch? *Probably ain't the time to get into it.*

Suddenly Dewmint panicked, rearing into the air, screaming, and kicking her feet out wildly. Andrew grabbed the saddle horn, terror clearing his mind and sharpening his breathing. Whadda I do? *Dismount. Let Dewmint go.* Are you crazy? *Can't outrun dust devils. You want her to die?* No, damn it! But I don't want me to die either, not here, not in your body! *Ain't gonna die, boy.*

Andrew tried to calm Dewmint as he quickly dismounted, then he smacked her on the rump, and she tore off through the swirling dust. What now? he asked, turning in a circle. He was surrounded by a thick grey dust, and he couldn't see anything past it. *Dust devils only got one weakness, a black spot near their center. Aim for it.* What about the wind witch? What's her weakness? *Ain't a she; a tumbleweed. But ain't a tumbleweed.* What the hell's a tumbleweed? *Not the time boy. Get ready.*

Andrew looked left and right, trying to see the dust devils or the wind witch, anything. At first all he could see was dirt, but then he saw them, shapes in the dust. Large, ominous shapes. Shapes twisted together with dust, rocks, and twigs. The air moved in small waves around him, almost as if the dust was breathing.

Andrew's hands shook, but he pulled a six-shooter and loaded it quickly. What now? *You're gonna have to aim real careful. They're gonna come at you, and it's gonna hurt, but don't fire. When you see a black spot, aim there. Do you hear me?* Yes, I hear you!

Andrew turned slowly, looking for something, anything, to shoot. There were dozens of distorted shapes surrounding him, but he couldn't see a black center in any of them. Suddenly the shapes began to move, and one tore into him so fast he barely saw it, but he felt it ripping across his leg. He jerked and pointed his gun towards it, but it was already gone. *Not yet!*

Pain shot through his shoulders as something tore across his back. Andrew bit his lip and held himself still. He could do this. He just had to wait for the right moment. He ignored a slash across his arms and fixed his eyes on one shape, watching it carefully. As it started moving towards him, Andrew kept his eyes on it, ignoring the other one that ripped across his face, ignoring the pain in his legs and back.

The dust devil came closer and closer, and suddenly Andrew saw it. Just a tiny bit of black in the center of a grey mass of dirt and thorns. He aimed and fired, and dust spewed everywhere, coating Andrew in debris. He fixed his eyes on another one. They were attacking so fast now Andrew felt like he was a speed bag. He could barely catch his breath before another hit him, and every time one tore across him, his body cried out in hot pain. He swiped blood out of his eyes and fired again. A dust devil exploded.

He fired again and again, reloading and reloading, until he ran out of ammo, and then he pulled one of his knives. His whole body stung. Blood was oozing into his palm, but he just gripped the knife tighter. He only had two knives, so he knew he couldn't throw them. He'd never be able to find them again, and then he'd be weaponless. The absolute pure fear and dread that clawed at him sharpened everything, making everything clearer. He wasn't going to die like this. Not in Pecos's body. Not here. Not now.

He waited until a dust devil was almost on him, and then he lunged for its center, plunging his knife into it. The dust devil exploded, tearing skin off Andrew's hand as it did. He lunged at another and another. He could barely see but he kept stabbing at little black dots.

Suddenly it was quiet. Dust hung in the air like a curtain, blocking his view. Andrew turned slowly trying to find the next one, but he couldn't see anything. He turned faster, searching, looking. *Be still,* Pecos ordered. What? *Be still. There! On the left!* Andrew turned.

A large mass towered over him, and Andrew's heart stuttered in his chest. He stumbled backwards staring in disbelief as the remaining dust devils merged to form one huge dust monster. *Find your feet, boy! You gotta be fast.* Andrew grabbed his other knife with his left hand as the dust devil monster moved toward him. The twigs had twisted into a face of sorts, and it was snarling.

I can't! I can't fight this! I'll never win! *Focus!* No, look; it's huge; I can't, Pecos. You! You do it! Take over; kick me out; you've got to kill this thing! Andrew took a panicked breath and backed away from the monster, but there was nowhere to go, and he knew he couldn't outrun it. He'd have to fight. He really was going to die in Pecos's body. *Told you, boy, I can't! When you sleep I rip at you tryin' to get you out. Only fight I've ever lost, but we ain't gonna lose this one.*

Andrew tried to believe Pecos. He gripped his knives tighter, trying desperately to force air into his lungs, but the air was tight and thick around him. Without warning the monster rushed him, and Andrew dropped to his knees, stabbing his knife into the black center nearest him. The monster stumbled, but another dust devil replaced the one Andrew had killed.

Andrew stabbed left and right, right and left; some parts exploded, but others he missed. Dirt, debris, and twigs crashed into his face and body, ripping at him, tearing at his flesh, tearing at his whole being. But he couldn't give up; he couldn't quit fighting. Maybe he couldn't save anyone from that stupid snake, maybe he couldn't be Pecos Bill, but he could damn well save himself, because his mom needed him. And he wasn't going out like this!

He kept stabbing, ignoring his pain, and focusing on those tiny black dots, those tiny, little devil hearts, but something prickly suddenly grabbed him from behind, wrapping itself around his arms, holding him tightly, holding him still so the dust devil monster could shred him to pieces.

"What the hell?!" Andrew yelled, struggling. *Wind witch; snuck up on you. You gotta find my strength, boy!* The dust devil monster was pummeling Andrew with razor sharp punches. He felt his skin tear, but he tried to stay focused, knew he couldn't give into the pain and the fear.

"Boy! Where're you?" Charlie called out over the sound of the dust devil's howling.

Andrew opened his mouth to yell back, but he couldn't. His throat was too dry, coated in dust. He closed his eyes, trying to see Pecos's power, his strength, the liquid gold coursing through his veins, making him more. Please, Andrew thought desperately. Please help me.

He dropped to his knees, tearing his arms from the wind witch's grip, rolling to his feet, facing both of them, wishing he was stronger. The wind witch rushed him, thorny arms wide, and Andrew punched, trying to put everything he had into it, trying to punch through the wind witch, trying to obliterate it.

His fist hit the wind witch and kept moving, tearing through its spiky body, until his hand burst out the other side, and the wind witch collapsed to the ground with a shudder. *THAT'S IT, BOY!* Pecos yelled. Andrew didn't stop, but turned to face the remaining dust devils. If he had to punch every single last one of them to death, that's just what he was going to do.

A gun belt flew through the dust, landing at his feet, and Andrew dropped to his knees, grabbing the guns and firing into the dust devils as he moved. He fired and fired and fired. With each shot a portion of the dust devil monster exploded until with one final deafening shriek there was nothing but empty dust swirling in the air.

"BOY!" Joe yelled somewhere nearby. Andrew tried to turn towards his voice, but his strength was gone; he stumbled to his knees and fell to the ground.

Andrew dreamed. His dream was full of pain; everything and everywhere hurt. He was hot; he was cold. He was nothing.

The dream shifted, and he had won. He was Pecos. Not Andrew-Pecos, but Pecos. He could feel the strength inside him, filling him to the brim, and he was more, so much more.

He rode an enormous cougar over an icy mountain slope. The sky was pitch black, yet there was one bright star lighting his way. The cougar leaped a deep, narrow canyon and charged up the last slope, skidding to a stop on a jagged mountain peak. Snow glittered in the sparse light, and Andrew breathed deep; crisp cold filling his lungs. Then he howled. He howled at the sky, at the moon that wasn't there, at the bright lonely star, at the world.

The heat came again, and Andrew groaned in pain. He was Andrew, just Andrew; and he was on a baseball field. The ball was racing towards him, but Andrew could see the stiches, could see it spinning through the air. He readied his bat, knowing he'd knock it over the fence. He swung, and the bat hit the ball with a crack! The bat split in half, and the ball rocketed up, out, over the fence, and into the dark beyond. A grey cat meowed from the pitcher's mound.

It was cold, so cold, and everything was covered in ice. Andrew was covered in ice. The dark was everywhere. Cold and dark.

A twisting voice whispered, "Fail, fail, fail; you will fail. Die, die, die; you will die. Feed me!!!"

"PECOS!" Andrew screamed. "Where are you? Help me! It's so cold," he whimpered. "So cold."

Nothing. There was nothing. No pain, no cold, no heat. Just silence and grey all around. "ENOUGH!" Andrew screamed. "I wanna go home," he added in a whisper.

"Not just yet," a strangely familiar voice replied softly. "Not just yet."

Andrew woke gasping for air. "Easy, boy," Charlie said. "You're a bit banged up." Andrew looked around wildly, trying to remember where he was, who he was. He blinked in the brightness, finally recognizing Charlie, and it all came flooding back in vivid detail.

"Where am I?" he whispered.

"Not far from…well, anyway; you've been out a day and a half," Charlie replied.

"What?!" Andrew struggled to sit.

Charlie put a hand on his shoulder. "Easy. You need to rest." Andrew looked down. His clothes had been replaced with fresh, and his hands were wrapped in strips of bloody fabric. He touched his head and felt wet scabs on his forehead and cheeks.

"I can't believe I'm alive," Andrew whispered. "That really happened, didn't it? It wasn't a dream? There were dust devils and a wind witch." He shuddered, trying not to remember the feel of his flesh ripping.

"You did good, kid," Joe said softly. "Pecos and I faced off against some dust devils not long ago. They're wicked things." He looked Andrew square in the eyes. "That you're still alive says a lot about you. Not Pecos, you."

Doyle grunted, handing Andrew a cup of thick black coffee. "Never thought I'd be glad to see this," Andrew said, taking a deep sip. "Oh, that's good." *Damn right it is!* Pecos! We survived! *Yep.* Didn't die! *Nope.* Still alive! *Yep.* Andrew rolled his eyes, but smiled as he took another sip of coffee.

Chapter Fourteen

Andrew decided not to even try to stand until he'd drank at least three cups of coffee, maybe ten. He hurt all the way from his scalp to his pinky toes. If he'd thought he'd hurt before, he hadn't known what he was talking about. This was the true definition of pain. It even hurt to blink.

It ain't right, boy. You shouldn't be sore at all, Pecos growled in a frustrated tone. How can you say that? I was attacked by...dirt. And twigs. And a damn tumbleweed! Andrew stood carefully and walked towards the horses. *Don't matter. I don't get sore. It ain't...It ain't right.* Andrew rolled his eyes. Everyone gets sore sometime; maybe you just never noticed. Pecos didn't respond.

The coffee swirled through Andrew's body, warming it and shaking something loose in his mind. Something about all this was weird. He'd never heard of giant snakes or dust devils or wind witches or any of the other crap Pecos talked about. What if this wasn't his reality after all? What if it was some totally different reality? Like a different dimension or something. That was a thing, wasn't it?

"Joe," Andrew said, limping back towards the fire. "I'm lousy at history, but Christopher Columbus discovered the Americas, right?"

Joe stirred the fire with a long stick and shrugged his shoulder. "That's what some people say."

"A long time ago?" Andrew pressed.

"1492," Doyle snapped.

Andrew glared at Doyle for a second. Something about Doyle bothered him. It wasn't that he was mean or gruff; it wasn't that his face seemed to be carved from stone. There was just something…but Andrew couldn't quite put his finger on it. Andrew frowned. Joe was a little odd too. The way he held himself, the way he talked, the way dirt just didn't seem to stick to him.

"Why?" Joe asked.

"Why what?" Andrew had lost track of the conversation.

"Why're you asking about Columbus?"

"Oh, right. I'm just trying to figure something out. Where, I mean, when I'm from there aren't things like dust devils and wind witches and shamans running around. I thought maybe I'm not in my past, but some different past? You know, like a parallel universe?"

They stared at him like he was crazy. "What?" Andrew snapped. "It was just a thought!"

"I see your point," Joe said with a thoughtful nod. "But most people don't run into dust devils or wind witches, and if they did, they most likely wouldn't live to talk about it. So most people don't know about them."

"What're you saying?"

"I'm saying maybe there is stuff when you're from, you just don't know about it."

Andrew frowned, thinking about all the television shows and movies about things outside of comprehension; the supernatural, the spirit realm, the unknown. He'd even had a teacher last year who had made the argument that all myths, lore, and legends were based on some amount of truth, you just had to know where to look for it.

"Joe makes a valid point," a voice said from behind Andrew.

"Why're you here?" Andrew barked, turning to glare at the Grey Shaman.

"Wanted to see how you fared. First big fight and all."

"Really?"

"Really."

"Are you checking in on me or Pecos?"

"Does it matter?"

"I feel like it does," Andrew answered, wondering what the Grey Shaman was up to.

"Do you have a plan yet?"

"Pecos is working on it."

"He may want to hurry. You are getting closer."

Tell me somethin' I don't know, Pecos snapped.

"Septimis just turned east."

Didn't know that.

"So? Does it matter?" Andrew asked.

"He's right," Charlie said. "Just now."

"How do you know?" Andrew demanded.

"Just do."

Andrew growled under his breath. "I don't get it. What does it matter which way he's going?"

"More towns east, more people," Charlie said.

"Do you think Septimis knows that?"

"Maybe," the Grey Shaman said, "if he stopped to ask directions." He chuckled loudly, then disappeared.

"What?" Andrew asked. "I don't get it! What's going on?" *Shut up, boy! I gotta think!*

Andrew rolled his eyes and sighed simultaneously. He wished someone would just tell him what was happening or at least answer questions when he asked them. He stood and stretched, trying to relax his sore and aching muscles. *Quit that!* Quit what? *That stretchin'! I can't think when you're doin' that!* That doesn't even make sense. *Don't argue with me, boy!* Whatever.

Suddenly Andrew wanted to shoot something, anything, it didn't matter what; he wanted to watch something explode. He was just so sick of being treated like an idiot. "Doyle," he snapped, standing. "Let's go shoot something."

One of Doyle's eyebrows flew up, but he just nodded, and they walked out of the camp towards a mound of rocks. "Gotta be careful shootin' towards rocks," Doyle said looking around. "Bullets can ricochet."

"Rico-what?"

"Bounce back at you."

"Oh. That would be bad."

Doyle grinned fleetingly and pointed towards a dead stump. "We'll shoot at that."

"Do I have to jump over stuff and run and all that crap?"

"Not a bad idea, but nah, just shoot."

Andrew grinned, quickly loaded his six-shooter, and shot the dead stump into smithereens. It felt good to be good at something, even if he wasn't jumping around a corner or running, he could still shoot, and he could shoot pretty accurately too. He reloaded and shot again, watching as bits of the stump flew into the air, but suddenly his throat tightened and he couldn't breathe. The stump morphed into dust, and the bits flying through the air were twigs and rocks arrowing towards him. He gasped, searching for the black dot, dreading the feel of his skin ripping. He couldn't see it; he couldn't see it! Where was it?!

A warm hand wrapped around Andrew's hand, and Andrew swung panicked eyes around, meeting Doyle's cold, blue eyes. "Ain't nothin' there," Doyle said steadily.

Andrew looked past Doyle, saw the stump, saw the open, dust-free air, and knew Doyle was right. There was nothing there. He slipped his gun back into its holster and rubbed his hands over his face. Could he be more of an idiot? "I'm sorry," Andrew stammered. "I thought...I just...all the sudden..."

"Happens. Coffee?"

"Yeah," Andrew said with a short laugh. "That'd be good."

Dusk was coming, and Andrew, Doyle, Joe, and Charlie sat facing the falling sun, watching the colors spread across the trees and horizon.

"I felt it," Andrew said softly. "Just for a second, when I was fighting the dust devils, I felt Pecos's strength. It was there. It helped me. But I don't know how to hold onto it. And I can't fight Septimis if I can't use Pecos's strength."

"We'll figure it out," Doyle said.

Andrew shrugged and watched the orange spread to grey.

Listen up, boy! Pecos barked. *I gotta plan.* Really? *Yes really! I said so, didn't I?* Okay, what is it? *I'd tell you if you'd stop interruptin' me!* So tell me already! *Boy... As I was sayin'...You gotta call my brothers.* Call? *Howl! How, out of all the boys in the world, did I get stuck with you?* I don't know, and I can't howl. Pecos hissed in frustration, then said, *Fine; tell Charlie to find me a coyote.* Right now? *No, I ain't done! Stop interruptin' me!*

Andrew sighed and pretended to zip his mouth shut. *What was that for?* I zipped my mouth shut. *What?* Nothing; please just go on. *Humph. Anyway, we still need an army.* Why? *Well, as much as I hate to say this, we gotta have somethin' to distract that damn snake while you rope it.* While I rope it? Have you not been paying attention? I can't rope!!

You'd damn well better learn. It's the only chance we got. You'll spend tomorrow harnessin' my strength; then we ride. Andrew felt the blood drain from his face. They were doing this. They were really doing this. They were going to fight the humongous father of all snakes. And Andrew was supposed to rope him. He wanted to laugh, but he couldn't. *Got it?* Pecos snapped. Yeah. I got it.

"You alright?" Joe asked, handing Andrew a plate of food. "You look a bit green."

"Yeah, I'm fine." Andrew stared at the burnt biscuits. The smell of them made him want to vomit; he was so sick of biscuits. On the bright side, if the snake ate him, he'd never have to see biscuits again. He wondered if Doyle would notice if he only ate the meat and threw the biscuits in the fire. He sighed. Of course he'd notice. Doyle noticed everything.

"I guess Pecos has a plan," Andrew said slowly.

"What is it?" Doyle asked.

Andrew looked across the fire at them, wondering how four such different men had ended up working together. "Is this what you guys do all the time? Ride around fighting things?"

"We run cattle," Joe said. "You know that."

"Yeah, but where are they?! These cattle? Why aren't you out running them? Why're you here?"

"Some of the boys are taking a herd up to Abilene right now," Joe said. "As for this, who else is going to do it?"

"But why you? Why you four?"

Joe shrugged. "Just 'cause."

"Ain't no trouble in the world that can't find Pecos," Charlie said.

"That's true," Joe agreed with a chuckle.

"What does that mean?"

"Always somethin' findin' Pecos, or Pecos findin' somethin'," Charlie said. "Just the way he is."

"Huh." Andrew ate his food silently, wondering what his mom was eating, wondering if she was okay.

"So about Pecos's plan?" Doyle growled.

"Yeah. So he wants me to train tomorrow. He says I have to harness his power because apparently, in some alternate reality where I can actually rope, I'm gonna rope Septimis." *Boy...*

Andrew shook his head in disgust when the others nodded as if this somehow made sense to them. "And he told me to tell Charlie he needs a coyote?" Charlie nodded again. Of course Charlie knew what that meant. "Whatever, so that's it. The plan."

No one seemed bothered by the fact it wasn't actually a plan. It was a nothing, but they acted as if it made total sense. Andrew wanted to scream, but what would the point be?

"I'm gonna go for a walk," he mumbled, pushing to his feet and wandering off into the gloomy grey. He sat down on a stump a little bit away and stared sightlessly into the dusk. Then his eyes focused, and he gasped.

Never in his life had he seen the moon rise. It was amazing! The moon was so big, he felt like he should be able to touch it, and it was glowing, casting light over everything. When he'd first gotten here, he'd been too tired and scared to appreciate anything more than the amount of stars he could see. But now, now he could fully understand what Joe meant. He felt as if he'd never seen the moon before this moment.

"Glorious, is it not?" the Grey Shaman said as he sat beside Andrew.

"I hate that. It's so annoying. Couldn't you at least zap ten feet away or something?"

"Tsk, and do all that extra walking?"

Andrew snorted. "Why do you keep coming? Twice in one day even? You can't send me home; you don't know who brought me; you don't know how to kill the snake; why are you here?"

"Oh, but I do know how to kill Septimis."

"You do? How?"

"Easy. Pecos would be done with him in ten minutes, maybe twelve." Pecos growled. "Oh fine," the Grey Shaman said. "Five, on a good day."

Damn right. Andrew's shoulders slumped. For a minute there he'd thought the Grey Shaman was actually going to tell him something useful.

"Anyway, I come to speak to you. It is not every day I get the chance to speak with someone from a future."

"You mean THE future?"

"No; a future."

"Whadda you mean?"

"Andrew, Andrew, there are many possible futures. Thousands, millions, millions of millions, yours is but one."

"That doesn't make sense," Andrew insisted.

"Maybe not; but it is so. What seems to be the problem anyway?"

"What? What problem?"

"You seem to struggle as Pecos."

Andrew rolled his eyes. "I'm not Pecos."

"Clearly. Why not?"

"Because I'm Andrew! Duh. And apparently Pecos has this strength that makes him him, and I can see it, but I can't use it, not really. So I'm just me. Andrew Rufus. Sissy, momma's boy."

"Tsk, tsk. You are neither a sissy or…well, maybe you are a bit of a momma's boy."

"How would you know?" Andrew snapped.

"And Pecos is simplifying things. It is so much more than just strength."

"I don't see how that helps."

"It doesn't; just an observation."

Andrew growled, ready to shoot the Grey Shaman just because, but he was already gone. What'd he mean? he asked Pecos. *Don't know. Don't understand half of what that crazy old man says. This one time he gave me a pair of enchanted spurs.* Enchanted spurs? *He said there weren't no way I could lose my seat when I was wearin' 'em. The gall of some people! As if I need 'em!* Wait, you're mad 'cause he gave you something you didn't need? *Downright insultin' is what it was.* Andrew chuckled softly, leaning back so he could watch the moon pass through the sky.

Is it always like this? *Like what?* So…amazing! So beautiful. *Always. Damn near takes your breath away.* It really does; it really, really does. Andrew couldn't remember a single time in the city when his breath had been taken away by anything. When he tried to visualize his home, all he could see was grey with a few structured, blocked-in patches of green. It made him a little sad to think about it.

No one talked to Andrew when he walked back into camp. Probably because he walked right up to his saddle blanket, tucked it under his head, and closed his eyes. The others were doing their usual things. Joe was playing his harmonica, Charlie's eyes were closed, but Andrew knew he wasn't asleep, and Doyle was doing something with a piece of wood and a knife.

Joe was playing a cheerful song, and it reminded Andrew of his mom. He wished he'd been a little nicer to her when he'd seen her last. If he ever saw her again, he was going to hug her tight and beg her to cook him something edible.

He feel asleep smiling, imagining a plate of pancakes as high as the ceiling. In his dream, the syrup turned into blood, and the darkness crept out to devour it, pancakes and all. Andrew woke gasping. The fire was still dimly lit, the moon was high overhead, and Andrew could hear the others breathing.

He glanced around and saw Doyle watching him. "Don't you ever sleep?" Andrew hissed.

"You woke me," Doyle said softly. "Everything's alright. Sleep boy."

Andrew didn't argue, just closed his eyes. There was no point in trying to tell Doyle that nothing was all right. In fact, everything was wrong. It had been wrong for a long time. Long before he'd ended up here in Pecos's body. For a second he wished everything would go back to normal, to the days before his dad's new job, but there was a part of him, a very small part, that didn't want this to end yet.

He dreamed of baseball, but the entire other team was owls, and Andrew was the only player on his team. He pitched the ball, but the owls didn't bother to bat. Instead they chased him into the dugout and pecked at his face. He woke before dawn, hating sleep, ready to ride all night, every night, just so he didn't have to close his eyes again.

Chapter Fifteen

Andrew wasn't surprised to see Doyle already awake and brewing coffee. He took a cup gratefully, watching the moon slip beneath the horizon and the sun slip over it.

"So, how do we do this?" Andrew asked, taking a big sip.

"Well, the way I figure it," Doyle drawled, "You've been using at least a bit of Pecos's strength this whole time, whether you knew it or not."

"How do you figure?" Andrew asked, laughing.

"When you first got that rope, you could barely move it. Took you and Charlie both to get it on a horse. But you've been pullin' it down and puttin' it on without blinkin' for days now."

Andrew frowned, thinking back, and realized Doyle was right. He HAD been moving the Stone Rope on his own. How had he been doing that?

"Now, I've lifted that rope myself," Doyle continued. "And…it's a struggle. So you see what I mean?"

Andrew did see what he meant. He had been using Pecos's strength all along without realizing it, but how did that help? He needed to be able to use it when he needed it, not when it didn't matter.

"So all you have to do," Joe said, "is figure out how you did it."

Andrew laughed. "You guys make it sound easy."

"It is," Doyle said. "You already did it."

"Damn it! If it was that easy, I'd have been doing it this whole time!" Andrew jumped to his feet, stomped over to the Stone Rope, and tried desperately to yank it from the ground, but it didn't budge. *Just get outta the way!* How?! Tell me how, and I'll do it! Andrew knew he could lift the rope; he could remember doing it, but he just couldn't.

"So," Charlie said. "When he thinks 'bout it, he can't do it. When he don't, he can."

"Seems like," Doyle agreed.

"I'm right here, guys," Andrew said, sitting back down. "I need more coffee."

"I think you actually drink more coffee than Pecos," Joe drawled, twirling his mustache over his finger.

"So what if I do? I'm in pain, you know! My head hurts, my body hurts, look at all these cuts! I mean, I probably needed stiches." Andrew yanked the wrappings off his hands and gasped. "They're practically healed! How?"

"Just the way Pecos is," Joe said.

"Of course it is," Andrew snapped. *Boy, don't crack now. You can do this. You got somethin' inside you that keeps you goin', use it!*

Andrew frowned. Pecos was wrong. Andrew had never, not once, kept going when things got hard. He bailed at the first sign of difficulty. But he couldn't bail this time. People needed him.

"Okay," Andrew said with a sigh. "If I was in my time, I'd work out or something."

"Work out?" Doyle asked.

"Lift weights, run, do burpees, something like that."

"Lift weights, do burpees; what kinda crazy future you live in, boy?"

"I don't even know. Apparently it's A future, not THE future."

"What?" Charlie asked.

"I don't know; something the Grey Shaman said. Anyway. Let's get to this I guess." Andrew drained his coffee and stood. He was still sore, although considerably less sore than yesterday. He leaned over and touched his toes. *I hate it when you do this. Makes me look like a sissy fool.* At least you're a limber sissy fool. *That ain't funny, boy.* Is to me, Andrew snickered.

When he'd finished stretching, he looked around for a big rock. When he found a rock he figured no normal person could lift, he walked over to it and wrapped his arms around it. He breathed deeply, trying to feel the power in his arms, trying to will it into his fingers, and then he lifted. But he didn't. Because nothing happened. Okay, so maybe a smaller rock. *Don't get much smaller than that. Any smaller and you liftin' a pebble.* Ha, ha, ha.

Andrew tried lifting several different rocks, but he simply couldn't, not until the rocks were small enough that he could have actually lifted them in his own body. Doyle, Charlie, and Joe just watched him, sometimes making comments along the lines of "Even

I could lift that one". It was embarrassing and totally frustrating.

He gave up on rock lifting and tried pushups. He dropped to the dirt after six. How the hell much do you weigh, Pecos? *Just the right amount, boy.* This isn't working. Why isn't it working? *'Cause you're in the way.* Andrew sighed in frustration. If he could step out of the way, he certainly would.

He tried running around the camp, but tripped on his first step and face planted in the dirt. I hate your boots! How could you possibly run in these things? *Just do. And quit your whinin'. It ain't gettin' you nowhere.* I realize that. "Coffee," Andrew gasped, rolling over in the dirt and staring at the clear, blue sky. "I need coffee."

Doyle grunted and walked back towards camp while Charlie offered Andrew a hand and pulled him to his feet. "You're thinkin' too much," Charlie said. "Just let it go."

"Let what go?"

"Everything. You can't possibly do anything if the entire weight of all your worries is holdin' you down."

That was possibly the wisest thing Andrew had ever heard, but it was also the most useless. What was he supposed to do? Toss his worries into a river like a bunch of broken sticks? There wasn't a river for miles, and even if there was, it's not like he could actually pick up his worries. *Takin' it too literally, boy.*

Andrew sighed. "I'm just not good at this," he mumbled, rolling his fingers around a rock, clenching it, and throwing it for all he was worth.

"Did you see that?" Joe whistled. "Can't even see where it landed."

"What?" Andrew asked.

"The rock you just threw."

"Really?"

"Flew like a bird."

"Stop thinkin'," Charlie said. "Just do."

This was like knife throwing all over again. The harder Andrew tried, the worse he did. There had to be a way to get his mind out of the way. He took the cup of coffee Doyle handed him and sipped thoughtfully.

"Okay," Andrew finally said. "What about this; we'll talk about something."

"What?" Doyle asked.

"Yeah, I'll try to lift a rock, and you talk to me about something, something interesting. If I'm focused on you, maybe I won't be thinking about what I'm trying to do."

"Worth a shot," Doyle agreed.

Charlie and Joe went to feed and water the horses, and Doyle followed Andrew to a big rock. "Sure you wanna start with a rock that big?" Doyle asked doubtfully.

"Go big or go home, right?" *What?*

"What?"

"It's a saying…but I never really got it; my dad used to…oh, never mind. Let's just do this." Andrew wrapped his arms around the rock and nodded to Doyle.

"So, um, the six-shooters we got is new. Pecos tell you?"

"No."

"Yep, Pecos got 'em made special. Most cartridge revolvers aren't overly reliable or accurate, but these are every bit as good as black powder."

"Black powder?" Andrew strained to lift the rock. *Don't you know nothin', boy?* Not about guns. Ask me about baseball. *Don't care 'bout your baseball.* Whatever.

"Most guns you gotta put the stuff in separate; it don't come all together like your cartridges."

"For real?" Andrew asked, wondering how long it would take to load.

"Yep, these are real nice; heck of a lot quicker."

Andrew imagined trying to fight the dust devils with a black powder gun. He didn't think he'd have gotten very far. "How long does it take to reload?"

"Revolver, maybe two minutes; rifle, four times a minute if you're good."

"You're kidding! In two minutes I'd be dead!"

"That's what you got your knives for and your fists."

"Still."

"Don't drop that rock on your foot when you realize you're holdin' it, boy," Doyle drawled easily.

"What?" Andrew looked down, realized he was standing straight up, rock clutched to his chest. He'd been so busy thinking about reloading he hadn't even noticed he'd picked it up. "Oh crap! Whadda I do now?" *Toss it!*

Andrew wasn't sure he could. He knew he was holding it, knew he'd lifted it, but there was a part of his mind screaming at him, telling him it was impossible, telling him it was too heavy, telling him no one could lift such a huge rock. He shoved that part of his mind away and tried to throw it anyway.

It didn't make it far, maybe a foot, before it dropped to the ground like the enormous boulder it was. Andrew laughed in relief when it didn't roll back onto his feet. "I did it," he whispered. "I really did it." *Told you you could. Just gotta do it.* Andrew rolled his eyes. You know you're not always right. Look at the whole owl thing. *I was right; just didn't know they was gonna try to eat you.* Andrew laughed.

"Let's try it again," he said to Doyle. Andrew wrapped his arms around the rock, telling himself he'd already done it, he knew he could lift this rock. And then he lifted. "Damn it!" he hissed. "Why can't I do it?"

"So whadda you do back home?" Doyle asked.

"What?"

"You work or somethin'?"

"No; kids my age aren't really allowed to work."

"Why not?"

"Child labor laws and what not."

"Child labor what?"

"Laws. Anyway, I go to school. And when I'm not at school I hang out with Chuck and Ed. We play a lot of baseball. It's really the only thing I'm good at."

"Heard of baseball. How's it played?"

"There're two teams. One team tries to get a hit with the bat; the other team pitches the ball and tries to get the batters out. There's more to it than that, but that's the gist."

"Don't they run 'round in a circle or somethin'?"

Andrew laughed. "It's a diamond. If you hit the ball, you run the bases. There're three bases and a home plate. You have to get to home plate to score a point. I'm the pitcher for my team."

"You any good?"

"Yeah, pretty good."

"So you wanna drop that rock now, or you like holdin' it?"

"What? Oh." Andrew was holding the rock again. This was so frustrating. It's not like he could have a conversation with Septimis while he tried to rope him. He could feel the power coursing through his muscles, feel it helping him hold the rock, feel it warming his insides, and it felt amazing! He felt like he could actually fight something as big as Septimis.

He threw the rock, and it sailed a whole three feet before dropping. *Again.* "Let me try it on my own this time," Andrew said, wrapping his arms around the rock. He thought about his mom and the way she rubbed her hand through his hair, the way she called him "baby". It was strange he was missing all the annoying things she did.

It would be nice to be woken by a gentle, loving shake instead of a hard boot. It would be nice to eat a real meal of sausage and potatoes or fresh baked bread. *You got it, boy!* Really? He did! He was holding the rock. He closed his eyes and focused on holding it. The problem was when he focused on it, trying to do it, it was like the power ran away, but when he was somewhere else in his head, the power worked like it would for Pecos. It just did. He dropped the rock.

He lifted rocks all morning, but he never could figure out how to lift a rock without distracting himself first. When he sat down to eat with the others, he was tired, hot, sweaty, and completely discouraged.

"Can someone explain to me why it wasn't okay for me to kill the old owl dude, but we're actually trying to kill the father of all snakes, so like the oldest snake ever?" *For one thing, boy, the rope'll hold 'im still, so there's a chance if we give 'im a real good talkin' to, he'll wise up.* Seriously? Your actual plan is to talk to him? Did you see him?! *It's a long shot.*

"It's rare for an old one to kill the way Septimis is," Charlie said seriously. "Their age gives them wisdom most people and animals lack."

"So is the dark whisperer manipulating Septimis? Do you think we can get him to see reason?" Andrew asked.

"Thing is," Charlie said, "There was already hatred in Septimis's heart. The dark one just flamed it to life."

"How do you know that?"

"Hate don't come from nothin'."

Andrew supposed that made sense. If someone came along and told him all cats were incarnate evil, he would probably laugh. But, if they said all GREY cats were incarnate evil, he'd be inclined to believe it. "So what is the dark? What does it want?"

"Don't know," Charlie said.

"I know this is crazy," Andrew mumbled, feeling silly. "But in one of my dreams, it was saying 'feed me'."

Charlie shrugged. "There're legends of spirits that feed off death. Maybe this is one. Could be feedin' off the people Septimis kills."

That was a horrible notion, but it would also explain why the dark had bothered to wake Septimis. "Do we have to kill it?" Andrew asked, dreading the answer. How did one kill a dark spirit? Was that even possible?

Charlie just shrugged, stood, and walked off into the stubby woods. "Hey," Andrew said. "Where's he going?"

"Don't know," Joe answered. "Let's work on your roping."

"Those are my least favorite words of all time."

"Really? What about 'snake in your boot'?"

"I don't know," Andrew replied seriously. "Is it a poisonous snake?" Doyle laughed sharply. "Am I gonna be hunted by owls AND snakes if I end up killing Septimis?"

Joe shrugged. "Who knows? Let's go rope."

"Rather have the snake," Andrew muttered, pushing to his feet and retrieving his rope.

Andrew tried to throw the rope a couple times, but missed horribly. "Let's try distracting you," Joe said. "Worked with the rock."

"Okay. Why do you play the harmonica so much?"

Joe laughed. "Pecos got it for me not long after we first met."

"Really? Pecos got you a present?!"

"Not really. He said my singing was so terrible it scared the cattle, but I wouldn't stop so he got me a harmonica."

"Well I've never heard you sing," Andrew said, swinging the rope over his head, "But you play really great." He let the rope go and watched as it sailed out, missing his target by more than twenty feet. "I don't think that worked," he sighed.

"Sure didn't. Your twirl's good, your release looks good, but somewhere between the release and the object something goes haywire," Joe said as he picked up Andrew's rope and looked at it. "Try my rope."

"Okay." Andrew tried Joe's rope and Charlie's rope and Doyle's rope, but he didn't do any better. He could get the rope to go in the general direction he wanted, most of the time anyway, but that was it.

This ain't good. Entire plan hinges on you bein' able to rope. Come up with a new plan then! *There ain't no other plan, boy; this is it!* I'll keep trying. *Don't think 'bout the rope; think 'bout what you're tryin' to rope.* Okay?

Andrew twirled his rope into the air and focused on the stump he wanted to rope. He imagined it was a cow trying to run away. He only had a general idea of what a cow looked like, so he made it into an owl instead. He released the rope, and it sailed past the owl landing with a thump behind it.

Chapter Sixteen

Andrew shook his head with disgust and took a break to work with his knives. He hid behind a tree and popped out, throwing his knife as he ran towards another tree. He was getting better; and if he just ran with it and pretended he was playing a game with Chuck and Ed, he could feel the power swirl through his fingers, guiding him, pushing the knife farther and farther.

After his tenth successful hit, Andrew switched to guns for a while, trying to mimic his knife actions. He did pretty well; probably from all the water gun fights he'd trounced Chuck at. Andrew popped over a log, shooting two holes into a dead stump, rolled to the side, jumped to his feet and shot two more holes as he ran forward.

He grinned widely. *Not bad, boy, but it ain't gonna work with Septimis.* I know, Pecos, Andrew thought with a sigh, holstering his gun and picking up his rope. He twirled it over his head; he released it. It flew through the air and landed on a clump of grass, five feet past what he'd been aiming for. He aimed further out. It landed twenty feet short.

Why is this rope so long anyway? he thought agitatedly. *You never know. Might need to rope a train or somethin' real big, like, well I don't know, like a big damn snake!* Andrew rolled his eyes. A train, really? Andrew could almost feel Pecos shrug. Andrew shrugged too. Maybe Pecos really had roped a train. If anyone could, it would be him.

After another hour or so, Andrew needed a break. A coffee break. *Maybe you drink a bit too much coffee, boy.* Nah, no such thing, is there? *Not sure 'bout that.* Who cares? I want some coffee. He walked back to camp, saw the pot of coffee already simmering on the fire, poured himself a cup, and sat beside Doyle.

"So what're you doing?" he asked, sipping the coffee carefully.

"Huh?"

"With the wood."

"Oh," Doyle stared at his hands for a moment. "Whittlin'."

"Whittle-what?"

"Whittlin'. Carvin'." Doyle held up a bird that was only half-finished. Its wings were going to be spread out, and Andrew could tell right away it was a raven in flight.

"Wow! That's good."

Doyle grunted and kept on whittling. Little bits of wood dropped to the ground at his feet. "I don't think I ever saw a raven before I got here," Andrew said. Doyle grunted again. "Course I never saw a horse or a bear either. Or an owl. Not for real; not up close."

"Got a point, boy?"

"Nope; just making conversation."

"Make conversation with Joe."

"Okaaay..." Andrew stood and walked several steps away. He'd thought he'd been making progress with Doyle. He'd even seemed, if not nice, not not nice a couple of times. *Don't mind Doyle; just Doyle.* Yeah, Andrew thought, pushing away a twinge of hurt.

He walked over to the horses and started brushing Dewmint. She nuzzled his side, and he rubbed his hand softly over her velvety nose. He was certain he'd never felt anything so soft. He traced the white star on her forehead absently, breathing deeply.

Everything was so much more here. The stars were brighter, and there were more of them. The moon was bigger. The sun was hotter. The horizon was longer. Andrew simply felt more. The coffee tasted so rich, and the biscuits so dry. When they were riding the dust smelled and tasted like dirt, dirty dirt. And there were so many more sounds. Birds, those prairie dog things, the croak of the ravens. Andrew didn't know if it was just because he was experiencing everything for the first time or if Pecos's body just felt everything so much more.

"You're my favorite," he whispered to Dewmint. She nuzzled him, and he smiled. When he was riding Dewmint, he actually felt like he could do it, like he could ride a horse without falling off. It wasn't quite as easy with the other two.

When he had finished brushing her, he quickly brushed his five other horses so they wouldn't feel left out. Then he went to try roping again. He'd just started twirling when he heard a low growl behind him. Andrew dropped his rope and turned slowly, hand just above his gun, which didn't have any bullets in it. Maybe Pecos was right. It was useless if it wasn't loaded. Andrew's eyes widened when he saw a huge coyote standing behind him, hackles raised and teeth bared.

Oh crap, Pecos! It knows I'm not you! *Course he does! He ain't stupid. Where the hell's Charlie?* I don't know! Just then Charlie stepped between the trees and out into the open. *Tell Charlie to tell 'im everything's alright.* What? *Just do it!*

"Charlie, Pecos wants you to tell the coyote everything's alright?"

Charlie nodded and looked at the coyote. They stared at each other for a moment before the coyote's hackles relaxed, and it sat down, staring at Andrew with an open expression. What in the burnt biscuits? Andrew thought. *What?* Oh, it's an expression I made up on account of Doyle's biscuits...well, you get it. *Burnt biscuits. Kinda like it,* Pecos said with a chuckle.

If the coyotes can round up some animals for our army, I'd appreciate it. Okay, but what's in it for them? *Just tell 'im the same thing that makes the dust devils whispered in the snake's ear.* What? *Damn it, boy; just do it!*

"Pecos says we need an army, so he'd like you, Mr. Coyote, to round up some other animals. He wants me to tell you that the same thing that makes dust devils whispered in the snake's ear."

The coyote's face changed, and he was soon growling again. Andrew stepped back cautiously. "I just told you what Pecos said to say."

The coyote looked at Charlie, then turned, slipping away through the brush.

"He'll do as you ask."

"Okay, but I'm confused. How do we know they're the same thing? And why would the coyotes care?" *Don't know for sure; just a guess.* You don't know for sure?! You lied?! *Well, you're the one who actually said it.* Yeah, but I used your lips! Pecos chuckled.

"There're many animals the coyote won't be able to talk to; we should gather more messengers," Charlie said softly.

"What about the ravens?"

Charlie frowned. "Ravens don't usually listen to me, but I'll try."

"So you can, what, talk to animals?"

"Not the way you're thinkin', but yes."

"Wow. That's…wow." The entire world as Andrew had understood it was wrong. Or just not right. Or unclear. Could people still talk to animals? Were there magicians or shamans who could just zap from one place to another? Were there talking animals? And if there were, where were they?

"I'll see what I can round up," Charlie said.

"Hey, how far away is the snake?"

"Couple days maybe."

"How do you know?" *If Charlie says it's so, it's so.* Andrew rolled his eyes. Why? *Just is.*

"Just do," Charlie said at the same time.

Andrew shook his head, annoyed. "How come you never follow a road, but you always know where you're going? And how do you always know where to find water?"

Charlie grinned widely. "Just do," he said again with a wink, then he turned and faded into the woods.

Andrew hissed in agitation. Well, if they could "just do", he was going to "just do" too. And then he could say stupid crap like "just do" when they asked him how he did something super cool. *That don't make no sense, boy.* Stop listening to my thoughts! *My head.* I don't care; I'd like a little privacy, okay? *I'd like my body back.* Well, tough, and stop complaining; you sound like a sissy. *Boy...* Pecos... *Humph.*

I'm gonna run there, Andrew thought, staring at a hill a ways off. Pecos could do it; so I can too. I'm the wind. I'm Pecos. Andrew tried to let everything go, his fear, his embarrassment, his understanding of reality. He breathed in deeply, reaching his hands towards the sky, then breathed out, trying to push every thought out of his mind.

And then he ran. At first it wasn't much different than any other time he'd run, except Pecos's body felt heavier and more awkward. But he tried to imagine the power inside him, flowing through him, and suddenly he felt lighter and faster. He pushed harder, looking towards the top of the hill and imagining he was already there.

He dashed through the trees, moving faster than he'd ever moved before, feeling the air rush past his face, and the power moved with him, pushing him harder, urging him on. He could feel it flowing around him, like he'd been a dam standing in its way, and he tried to step aside and let it through.

He ran and ran and before he knew it, he had crested the hill. He tried to stop, but his feet were moving so fast he couldn't, and instead he tripped, went flying head over heels, and crashed into a juniper tree. Dirt and tree bits flew everywhere.

WHOHOO! You did it! Pecos shouted excitedly.

Andrew didn't respond, just tried to catch his breath, tried to see if anything was broken, and wondered how a man could run so fast. He finally crawled out from under the broken tree and dusted himself off.

"That was...awesome!" he exclaimed. "Let's do it again!" *Atta boy!*

Andrew ran down the other side of the hill and back up. His feet moved so fast he felt as if he was barely touching the ground. "I can't believe this!" he shouted as he careened to the top of the hill again. He accidently ran into a broken limb, tripping over it and landing hard on his face.

He swiped the blood from his lip and rolled to his feet laughing. "I'm the fastest man alive!" *My body, boy. And I ain't. There's at least one faster.* No way! *Yep. Met 'im once when I was out west on a cattle drive.* This is insane! Andrew sat down on a stump and just laughed. Partly because the world was so crazy, and partly because he was so relieved he'd finally learned to use Pecos's power.

He just barely, over the sound of his own laugher, heard the soft flutter of wings behind him, and he jumped to his feet, pulling his gun and spinning around. "Crap biscuits," he hissed. *What's that?* Um…variation of burnt biscuits. *Huh.* He was surrounded by owls. And not just the kind he'd seen inside Owl Haven, but many different kinds. Their eerie eyes pinned him in place.

One small owl stepped forward. "You killed one of our old ones," it accused.

"In my defense," Andrew stuttered, wishing he'd loaded his guns, "he was gonna eat me."

"Regardless. We have come for your blood. Blood for blood; but we will wait. Pecos did not kill Black Beak. You did. We will wait." And with that, the owls hissed at him and winged into the sky.

Andrew shuddered. "That was super creepy. Are they seriously gonna wait until you and I are separate?" *Seems like.* Good, I guess?

Andrew flipped his gun open and loaded it, slipping it back into the holster, and pulling out another gun to load. I hate to say it, but you were right. *Of course I was. 'Bout what?* Useless if they're not loaded. *That's just a given.* See if I tell you you're right again. *But I am.* Andrew sighed. Pecos was the most annoying person he'd ever met or not met. *I heard that!* Good.

When Andrew was done loading his guns, he looked around for a big rock. He wanted to lift it without being distracted. He was sure he could do it now. Something had changed; he wasn't sure what. It was as if the power was working with him, allowing him to use it even though he wasn't Pecos.

He found a large rock and wrapped his arms around it. I need to lift this rock, he thought. *What the hell you doin'?* Telling the power what I need. *What? How hard did you hit your head when you fell?* Andrew rolled his eyes and visualized lifting the rock. It was heavy, and at first he couldn't, but then the power moved and the rock was in his arms. He grinned, ecstatic that he'd finally done it, finally figured it out, but then his grin faded. Strength or no strength, he still couldn't rope.

Andrew dropped the rock and glanced around him. He had been so excited to finally channel Pecos's power, he hadn't noticed that the sun had already gone down. The moon wasn't up yet, and it was growing dark. Very dark. He wasn't scared of the dark; he really wasn't. He was scared of that voice, that thing, that spirit or being that lived in the dark and breathed blackness and death.

He turned toward the others, running down the hill as quickly as possible, and skidded into camp, stumbling slightly and almost tripping into the fire.

"Whoa, boy," Joe drawled. "Might want to slow it down."

"No way! Did you see? I'm doing it! I'm using Pecos's strength."

"Good. Now maybe you can find his aim."

Andrew's shoulders slumped. "The cup's always half empty with you guys."

"Half a cup of coffee's better than none," Doyle stated.

"No, I didn't mean…oh never mind. Give me a full cup though. I need it."

Chapter Seventeen

Charlie didn't return until it was totally dark. "I've spread the word," he said simply, before sitting down and filling a plate with food.

"So what now?" Andrew asked, refilling his coffee cup.

"What does Pecos say?" Joe asked.

Pecos? *It's time.* Time for what? *To fight.* You sure? Andrew asked, feeling a frisson of panic. I can only barely use your strength, I still can't rope, and we don't know if the army's coming. Maybe we should wait. *Few days, few towns. Worth it?* What? *You gonna learn enough in a couple days to make it worth all the people who're gonna die for it?*

Andrew paled. All the time he'd spent training, riding, sleeping, and recovering from the dust devils more people had been dying. Because of him. All those deaths, all those children. Because of him.

If he wasn't here, Septimis wouldn't have made it past that town where they first saw him. He wouldn't even have gotten to that town because Pecos would have ridden through the night. All those people had died because Andrew was weak. He couldn't fight; he couldn't aim a rope; he couldn't do anything. He wasn't Pecos.

He had never felt so completely useless in all his life. Guilt swamped him, because part of him, a very small part, had been having fun, and more people had been dying while he'd been having an adventure. I'm so sorry, he thought. He wasn't telling Pecos, he was telling them, all the dead people, those people who would never see the moonrise again.

But he still wasn't ready. He wanted just another minute. "We'll sleep a few hours; then we ride," Andrew said, ignoring the fear that felt like it was choking him. He grinned crookedly. "We've got a snake to fight."

The others nodded, then Charlie leaned his head back and closed his eyes, Joe pulled out his harmonica, playing a sad, lonely song, and Doyle slipped a piece of wood from his pocket. Andrew wanted to close his eyes and go to sleep, but he didn't think he could. He'd thought about riding right out, but he wasn't quite ready. He'd never ridden into battle before, not like this, not a planned battle. And everything was riding on him and his ability to be Pecos Bill, legendary cowboy hero. It was laughable.

Andrew startled as Doyle settled beside him. "Best not think 'bout it," Doyle drawled. "Just another night; just like any other night."

Andrew nodded. "Charlie said the snake's still a couple days away." He stared at the orange flames curling around black wood. "I can't rope," he whispered.

"Maybe you can't, but Pecos can." Andrew felt like screaming. It wasn't that easy. It wasn't! Why did they think it was? "Finished that raven," Doyle said, opening his hand to reveal a small wooden raven and handing it to Andrew.

Andrew turned it over in his hands. "It's amazing! It looks just like a real raven. How do you do it? Never mind. Just do."

Doyle chuckled softly. "You can keep it."

"Really? Thanks; it's awesome!" *Shut up, boy!* What? *We don't gush.* Gush? I wasn't gushing. *Damn near.* Andrew rolled his eyes and looked more carefully at the raven. It had an incredible amount of detail for something so small. It was even black. He wanted to ask Doyle how he'd made it black, but he knew Doyle didn't liked being asked questions so he just slipped it into one of his vest pockets.

He tried to count how many days he'd been here, but everything blurred together. He thought maybe it had been seven or eight, but he couldn't be sure. It was hard to believe that in that short of time he'd learned to ride a horse, gotten into a fist fight, learned to shoot and throw knives, almost been killed by dust devils, and ran so fast it was unbelievable. If his mom had any idea what he was up too, she'd faint. And then she'd lock him in his room for the rest of his life.

"Get some sleep, boy," Doyle said, standing and walking back to the other side of the fire.

Andrew tucked his saddle blanket under his head and gazed at the stars and the enormous moon moving among them. The air was still warm, and insects were buzzing and chirping all around. The fire snapped, and Andrew grinned slightly. The glowing warmth of the fire and the men sitting around it pushed his fear back and for the moment, for just a moment, he felt safe.

He fought dust and twigs in his dreams. Every time he aimed for the black spot it moved and he missed. Suddenly the black spots came together, twigs dropping to the ground, and the spots formed a gigantic black monster with sharp, black teeth and a gaping mouth. And he was just Andrew, not Pecos, so it swallowed him whole, and he woke, gasping for air and struggling to break through the darkness.

The light from the fire was dim, but the moon illuminated everything. There was no dark, and he was safe. He glanced across the fire and saw the others watching him. "Guess it's time, huh?" he said with an awkward laugh.

They stood without a word and saddled their horses. Andrew tried using Pecos's strength as he threw his saddle over Peppermint. At first he struggled with the Stone Rope, but he knew he could do it, he knew he could, so he forgot he couldn't and lifted it onto Babe's saddle. Charlie put out the fire, and they mounted, riding silently towards the dark, towards Septimis, towards death.

As soon as the sun peaked over the hills, Andrew unraveled his rope and started practicing. The landscape had changed during the night. They'd left the sparse forest behind and were riding through plains or prairies, Andrew wasn't sure which. It looked like a desert to him, but when he'd asked, Pecos had snapped "ain't the desert, boy", so Andrew didn't dare ask what it really was.

He could throw the rope far and in the general direction, but it was always off one way or another. Too far, too short, too left, too right. Andrew tried to feel the power as he threw, tried to push it into his arms, tried to visualize the rope slipping over his target, but it didn't help. Whatever the power was, it didn't actually make him Pecos. He was still Andrew, just Andrew who could be stronger and faster if he focused.

He roped all day, and he didn't improve. *Seen girls rope better than you,* Pecos snarled. Then I hope you get a girl next time! *Boy...* Andrew rolled his eyes and kept trying. His back and shoulder ached horribly, but he didn't stop, he couldn't stop. People depended on him being able to do this.

When he couldn't move his arm anymore, he put the rope away and rode up next to Charlie. "Have you ever seen the dark?" Andrew asked.

"Nope," Charlie said.

"Has Grandma?"

"In visions."

"Has it always been here?"

"There're stories and legends, passed down from the elders of a darkness that stalks the earth and hunts for prey. But legends're tricky. Could mean a cougar or a bear. Could mean a man or a people."

"Oh. Are there other old ones, like first ones?"

"Yep."

"Have you ever met one?"

"Only in a dream."

"Which one?"

"Town up ahead."

"A live town or a dead town?" Andrew whispered, dread filling him.

"Dead."

"Can we go around it?"

"Someone's still alive."

Burnt, crap biscuits, Andrew thought, wrapping his reins around his hands and struggling not to ride the other way. He looked for the town, but he couldn't see it. All he could see was a swarm of large black birds, circling in the sky.

"What're those birds?" he asked Charlie.

"Vultures. They follow death."

"Whadda you mean?" Andrew asked, but Charlie didn't answer.

They rode towards the town silently, except for the soft plod of their horses' hooves. Andrew wished he could close his eyes; he hadn't actually seen that first town after Septimis had plowed through it. He didn't know what he'd see, but he could guess.

The blood left his face, leaving him cold, when the town came into view. The only way he could tell a town had ever stood there was the road that started into it and the piles of wood and stones strewn across the area where the town had been.

Charlie dismounted and started walking through the debris, and the others followed him. Andrew took his time dismounting, wishing he could just ride away. He walked carefully between the broken boards, ignoring the splotches of brown he occasionally glimpsed, knowing they were once bright red. He gasped and tripped when he almost stepped on a hand sticking out from under a bit of board. It wasn't a large hand; it was small, like a child's.

Andrew started to pull the boards away, looking, searching. *Boy, if Charlie didn't stop...then...ain't alive.* You don't know that! Andrew snapped, tearing a long board out of the way. *Boy... I have to check!* He pulled on the arm slightly to see which way to dig and gasped, forcing bile down his throat as the arm pulled free from the rubble. He dropped it, staring in horror. He'd failed. The child was dead. This was only an arm; the rest of the child was lost somewhere under the rest of the town.

Boy, I... I don't wanna talk about it Pecos. You were right, okay? *I don't...I mean...* Shut up! Andrew swiped a tear from his eye and stumbled after the others, closing his eyes to anything he might see, stepping around the body of a crushed man, looking anywhere but there, wishing he'd stayed with the horses.

When he caught up with them, they were standing around the torso of a man. The rest of him was caught under what must have been half a house. Andrew just hoped the rest of him was there. He assumed this was the live one Charlie had mentioned; and it was, because his eyes popped open when Charlie touched him.

"Liza," he gasped. Charlie shook his head, and the man began to weep. "Liza, my Liza," he sobbed, grasping Charlie's arm. "Kill me," he managed between sobs. "Please...kill me."

Andrew stepped forward. "We can help him, Charlie. We can get him out!"

"NO!!!" the man screamed. "Kill me! If you won't, just leave me be!"

"But...I...but..." Andrew stammered. Doyle grabbed Andrew's arm and pulled him away, back towards the horses. "Doyle, no!" Andrew argued, struggling against Doyle's iron grip. "We can save him! I can lift the boards! I can do it! Please let me help him." He hadn't been able to save the child, but the man, he could save the man.

Doyle paused, staring hard at Andrew. "Can't save someone who don't wanna be saved, boy."

"But I can!"

"No." Doyle looked past Andrew for a moment, face dark. "He don't wanna be saved. Might save his body, but you can't save his soul."

Charlie and Joe caught up to them, and Andrew paled. "Did you?" he gasped. Charlie nodded and walked past him. Tears streamed down Andrew's cheeks. They could have saved him. So many dead, but they could have saved that one.

Doyle's right, boy. He didn't wanna be saved. Better this way. How can you say that? Andrew stumbled after the others, blind to the dead and broken bodies; cold numbness creeping over him. *Gotta have somethin' to live for. That man wouldn't have lived, even if you'd pulled 'im out.* You don't know that! *But I do.*

Andrew shook his head, brushing his hand over his eyes and blowing his nose on his sleeve. Pecos didn't yell at him, but Andrew wished he had. If Pecos had yelled at him for not using his hanky, maybe just maybe Andrew would feel something besides this terrible emptiness.

He started to walk forward, but stumbled when he saw the red-headed vultures everywhere, crooked beaks grasping at flesh and ripping it from the bones. One vulture was tearing at the arm Andrew had unearthed.

"No!" Andrew snapped. "Stop that!" He ran towards the birds flapping his arms and screaming. The vultures scattered, but just settled somewhere else, ripping at some other piece of flesh.

"STOP IT!" Andrew screamed, running at them again. These were people; they deserved respect. They should be buried, damn it, not lying out in the sun to rot and be eaten by birds. "GO AWAY!" he yelled, chasing after them.

You can't stop 'em, boy. Sure I can! *How? By chasing 'em all day?* If I have too! Andrew picked up a loose board and chucked it into a group of birds pecking at the crushed body of a woman. *We gotta go.* Shut up!

Andrew threw another board and another. "GET OUT OF HERE!" he yelled.

He jumped when a hand grabbed his shoulder. "Leave them," Joe said firmly.

"Leave them? These are people! They deserve better than this!"

"They were people. They're not here anymore. Vultures, they clean everything up. It's all part of the order."

"The order's stupid then!" Andrew yelled.

"Maybe," Joe said with a shrug. "Thing is, these people are gone. You can't save them. There're other people out there, people who haven't died yet, and them you can save."

Andrew laughed bitterly. "I can't even stop these damn birds from eating anyone, what makes you think I can save anyone?"

"Just do," Joe said.

Andrew closed his eyes. Damn them and their "just do's".

"Let's go," Joe urged.

"Fine." Andrew dropped the board he was holding and turned his back on the vultures. Joe was right. He couldn't help these people, not anymore. He just hoped Joe was right about the part where he saved the other people. *Course he is!* Shut up, Pecos.

They rode all day in silence, even harder than before, but Andrew didn't care. He'd ride all night if he had to. He needed to end this. He didn't want anyone else to die because of him. He didn't want to see any more flattened towns or broken men and torn children. He wanted to kill a snake, the father of all snakes, and he didn't care if snakes hounded him for the rest of his life. It would be worth it.

When they rode slow enough, Andrew roped and roped and roped, but he never roped a thing. How would you have done it without the rope? he asked, feeling a little desperate. *What?* You didn't need the rope in the first place. You just went after the rope because of me. How would you have done it? And don't say "just would've" or I'll kill us both! Pecos chuckled softly.

Thing is, boy, I don't exactly know. I really do just do. I don't think it through or figure it out first. I ride in guns blazin'; if that don't work, I switch to fists. Andrew frowned. So you'd have beaten him to death? *If I had to. If it worked.* Damn it, Pecos! You're not helping! *How 'bout we just ride in there and see what happens?* That's not a plan! *Usually works for me.* I'm not you!

Andrew tried to think of a plan, any plan that would help him kill Septimis. He had to win, he just had to. He couldn't let Septimis keep killing people, crushing the life out of them, stealing their reason to live. Maybe the army would eventually come; maybe there was a chance the army could actually defeat Septimis, but Andrew couldn't wait. He simply couldn't let anyone else die.

He honestly didn't know why he cared. He'd never cared about anything before. But he did. He cared a lot. He felt the weight of all those people he'd failed to save. He felt the weight of their deaths, and he thought, maybe, just maybe, if he could kill Septimis, the weight would go away.

Before long the sun slid into the earth, and everything grew dark, but they didn't stop, just kept riding. They still hadn't talked; even when they had stopped to switch horses they hadn't said a word. But

Andrew didn't mind. He wasn't ready to talk to them yet. He didn't understand their version of right, wasn't sure he wanted to.

Dewmint suddenly reared, and Andrew jerked in surprise, looking around trying to figure out what had spooked her. He heard a horrible whistling sound behind him and froze. Dust devils! But it was dark! He'd never be able to see the black spot. They were going to get shredded.

"Dismount!" Andrew heard Doyle yell. "Protect the horses!"

Without warning pain flared across Andrew's cheek, and he jerked. His spare horses were whining and fighting against their leads, but Andrew dragged them forward, jumping from Dewmint and ignoring the whirling dust around him.

There were too many horses and not enough of them, but Andrew took his place beside Doyle and faced the dark, trying to see the dust devils, trying to see their weak spot. Whadda I do, Pecos? *Wait.* Andrew slowed his breathing and tried desperately to make out the shapes in the darkness. He felt the wind rushing towards him and braced himself, gun in hand, searching for that special spot, wishing the moon had risen, wishing there was even a hint of light.

A dust devil hit Andrew full force, knocking him against the horses, tearing the skin from his hands, but even that close, Andrew couldn't see its devil heart. A light suddenly flared behind them, and a bright, glowing fire filled the plain with light.

Andrew gasped. There were hundreds of dust devils surrounding them. One was tearing towards Doyle, and Andrew fired, hitting the spot and exploding the devil into formless dust. Andrew searched for another to kill and saw Charlie run from the fire and join them, pulling his bow from his back as he did.

Andrew fired again and again, waiting until the devils were right in front of him, until he could see, but there were so many. The horses behind them shrieked and bucked. Andrew was terrified they were getting torn to pieces, but he couldn't stop, couldn't check; he had to keep fighting.

A different sort of howl filled the air, drowning out the high-pitched, whirling of the dust devils, and dark, hulking shapes jumped from the blackness, hurling themselves at the dust devils, snarling and gnashing. *Brothers!* Pecos said fiercely, and Andrew realized they were coyotes.

Andrew fumbled with his gun, needing to reload, but a dust devil was right in front of him. He dropped his gun, ripping his knife from its sheath, and slammed it into the black heart. Twigs ripped past his hand and face as it exploded.

Another came, and he smashed his knife into it as well, flinching as it tore the skin from his fingers. The dust devils fell back, gathering together as they'd done before, growing and merging into one. The coyotes surrounded Andrew and the others, and they faced the devil monster together, waiting for it to move forward.

Andrew heard a loud whooshing and saw Joe release his rope. The rope flew through the air, and

Andrew watched in disbelief as it landed around the entire group of dust devils. Joe jerked, ripping the rope up, and the devils flew into the air. He jerked again, this time down, and the devils crashed into the ground with a horrendous crack.

Dust flew into the air all around them, and twigs rained from the sky, but when the air cleared all the dust devils were gone except one. The last one exploded as one of Charlie's arrows ripped through it, and absolute silence filled the night.

"How..." Andrew stuttered. "But...you...and then..."

"Make the boy some coffee, Doyle" Joe drawled. "He's lost his tongue."

"But..." Andrew didn't finish. He couldn't. Joe had just roped, ROPED, an entire group of dust devils to death. Was that even possible? Clearly it was, but still. How Andrew wished Joe could wield the Stone Rope. Joe was amazing at roping; he'd rope Septimis in seconds and then it would all be over.

Dewmint whinnied, and Andrew spun around. "You okay?" he asked softly, running his hands over Dewmint's side. She had a few cuts, but nothing serious, and his other horses were fine.

Andrew searched for the coyotes, but they were already gone. "Where'd the coyotes come from?" he asked.

"Been trailin' us for a day or so," Charlie said, picking his arrows from the ground and slipping them back into his quiver.

"Really? I give up," Andrew said, plopping to the ground near the fire. "I'm never gonna understand this place or you guys or anything." *Quit whinin', and drink your coffee.* Fine; I do like the coffee.

Chapter Eighteen

After they'd washed down some dried meat with coffee, Charlie looked at Andrew. "Wanna rest for bit?"

Andrew knew Charlie was only asking for him. If it was Pecos they would certainly keep riding. He may not get it, he may not get them, but they had a job to do, and they were going to do it. He wasn't particularly looking forward to sleeping, not after the town they'd passed through. In fact, he'd be all right if he never slept again, even if he was exhausted.

But he needed a minute. Not to sleep, but to try to use Pecos's strength. He wished he had a whole month to train, but he didn't. He'd take an hour though. "I wanna train for a bit, not long; then we'll ride."

Charlie nodded and leaned his head back, closing his eyes. Joe pulled his hat over his eyes and was snoring in under a minute. Doyle closed his eyes, but otherwise didn't move. Andrew didn't know if he was asleep or not, because he was sitting upright. Doyle still creeped Andrew out. He was just…scary.

Ha! You should meet Enrica. Now she's scary! Really? *Really!* Andrew walked a couple feet away and looked around for large rocks to lift. At first he struggled, but he breathed deeply, focusing on the warm pulsing energy inside him and tried again and again. Before long he was lifting the rock without fail; he just imagined himself doing it, and he did.

He tried to think how else he might fight Septimis. Pecos had said he'd use his fists, but Andrew didn't have anything soft to practice on. He'd once seen Chuck punch the floor, so he knew better than to walk around punching solid objects, even if he was in Pecos's body. He did some push-ups, just for kicks, managing thirty before he finally collapsed, which he felt was pretty good since he'd only ever managed fifteen in his own body, and he was way lighter.

Were you always this way? he asked, throwing a rock into the darkness, listening for the clunk of it landing, but never hearing it. *Far as I 'member.* I wonder why I don't have it. *Maybe you do.* I think I would've noticed. 'Sides, I'm not good at anything, and you're good at everything. *Maybe.*

Andrew guessed he was as ready as he'd ever be. He started to return to camp, but paused when he felt the air shift behind him. He cringed as he turned, hoping it was the Grey Shaman and not a bunch of owls.

"I am curious," the Grey Shaman said with a slight grin. "Why the rocks?"

Andrew sighed. "Pecos is right, you know." *Always, but 'bout what?* "Shamans," Andrew said with exasperation.

Grey Shaman chuckled. "I imagine if you were to meet an actual shaman, you might enjoy him, but why the rocks?"

"I'm trying to be Pecos."

"And?"

"The rocks help me focus the power."

"Ahhh."

"I'm not Pecos. I'm not. Can you really not send me home? Septimis is killing people, breaking them into pieces, and someone has to stop him. Pecos has a much better chance than I do!"

"You may surprise yourself," the shaman said mysteriously, before simply disappearing.

"I really don't like you," Andrew said to the empty air. *No one does. Most people run the other way.* We should start doing that. Pecos chuckled, but didn't respond.

Andrew walked back to camp to find the others still fast asleep. How can they fall asleep so fast, anyway? Never mind, don't tell me; I already know. Pecos chuckled again, just as Doyle's eyes popped open, and Andrew shook his head.

"Let's ride," Andrew said, waking the others, assuming they weren't already awake and watching him. *They were.* Of course they were.

They had been riding for a while when Joe dropped back to ride alongside Andrew. "You're doing good," Joe said. "It's a lot to take in."

Andrew thought Joe was really selling it short. It wasn't a lot to take in; it was a whole different world. It was reality turned on its head, but he knew Joe was trying to be nice, so he murmured, "Thanks."

"Something sure is rousing things up. Last time I saw dust devils was about a year ago, but I've never seen so many as there were tonight. Nasty creatures."

"What are they?"

"Normal ones are just swirls of dust caught in the wind. Like mini-tornados. But these, the carnivorous kind, they're alive somehow."

"Do you think Pecos is right? Do you think the dark is making them?"

"Don't know. Doing what's right isn't always simple or easy, especially out here," Joe said softly. "It's not like the city where there're rules for everything, even how you cross the street." Andrew grinned. Maybe time hadn't changed so much after all. "But you do what you do," Joe said with a shrug.

Andrew knew Joe was talking about the man Charlie had killed, but he didn't want to think about it. Was there really a version of reality where killing someone because they asked you to was right? How could it be? Maybe they couldn't have saved him. Maybe he was too messed up, but shouldn't they have at least tried?

"Is it easy where you're from?" Joe asked.

Andrew had always thought so. Everything was in clear shades of black and white. There was no grey. Was there?

Dawn was creeping over the land, and Joe smiled, pulling his watch from his pocket. He flipped the top and stared at the face for a moment before flipping it closed again. "My grandpa gave me this watch when I was about your age. To him it was about being a man, being strong, doing what needs done. And it is all of those things. But it's also time, in all its essence. This moment...this is the right moment."

Joe stared at the sun for just a minute before handing the watch to Andrew. "I want you to have it. It'll help remind you."

"Remind me of what?"

"Whatever you need reminded of."

Andrew frowned. All four of them were always spouting off wise sounding speeches or advice, but most of the time he didn't understand what they were saying. No one talked like they did. Or maybe just no one he knew. He didn't know any cowboys or warriors or whatever they were.

"Are you sure?" Andrew asked, slowly taking the watch from Joe. "It was your grandpa's."

"I'm sure." Joe grinned, then gently tapped his horse, riding ahead.

Andrew held the watch carefully. He'd never seen a watch like it before. The sun glinted off it, making it glow. He flipped it open like he'd seen Joe do. There was writing on the inside, and he squinted to read it. "The battle is not lost if you do not admit defeat." Andrew laughed out loud. Of course it wasn't. Only a bunch of crazy cowboys would believe that.

Crazy cowboys? Sure! You guys are all loco. *Who you callin' loco, boy?* I'm just messing with you, Pecos, Andrew thought, slipping the watch into a vest pocket across from Doyle's carving.

"Somethin' up ahead," Charlie called back.

Andrew cringed, hoping it wasn't another town. He rode up with the others. "What is it?"

"Not sure," Charlie said thoughtfully. "I think…I think it's snakes."

"Snakes? Like Septimis?" Andrew wasn't ready yet. He'd thought he had at least one more day. He'd thought maybe he'd come up with something like a plan.

"No…little ones."

They rode over the top of a small rise and pulled the horses to a halt. Spread across the valley in front of them was a huge mass of snakes, hundreds, thousands, maybe hundreds of thousands. And they weren't what Andrew would call little either. Some of them were huge, as long as a truck, longer; and they were all slithering and hissing, and they all looked mad. Andrew stared wide eyed. He'd never seen so many snakes in his life, hadn't known so many snakes even existed.

One of the largest snakes slithered forward, standing upright when it was just feet away. "The birds told us you go to fight our father," it hissed.

The others looked at Andrew. "I'm not Pecos," Andrew whispered. "You talk to it." Joe raised an eyebrow, and Andrew sighed. "Fine." He raised his voice. "Septimis is killing people! We have to stop him!"

"We do not go to war against humans when they trod our young into the dust and stretch our bodies over their boots."

"It is a little different," Andrew began.

"Why?! Do we not think? Do we not love?"

"I didn't mean like that!" Andrew snapped. "I meant because Septimis is literally trying to kill people, I mean that's his goal, to kill. He's just killing and killing."

"Man does not do this?"

"You're right; humans suck! Is that what you wanna hear? If some dude starts killing a bunch of snakes, it's totally fine with me if you form an army and kill him. He probably deserves it!" *Gettin' off track, boy.*

Andrew dismounted, even though every fiber in his body told him to run away. The snake was huge and standing up it was almost as tall as Pecos. It had a rattle and huge fangs hanging from its mouth, which meant, if he remembered right, it was poisonous.

"Look," Andrew said, holding his hands out to the sides. "I don't wanna fight you to get to him. I don't have a fight with you. In fact, I don't wanna fight Septimis. If he'll listen to reason, we don't have to fight."

"There's something else going on here!" Andrew shouted, hoping all the snakes could hear him. "Something tricked Septimis for its own reasons. Some kinda darkness that feeds on death, feeds on anger, feeds on terror."

"To stand aside would betray our father," the snake replied sternly.

"Hasn't there been enough death?!" Andrew yelled. "Do you seriously wanna add your own?" He didn't even like snakes, but he couldn't see the point in killing them. They weren't the problem. Septimis was.

Can we go around them? he asked Pecos. *Lose 'bout four hours.* Damn it! "GET OUT OF THE WAY!"

Andrew shouted. "I'm not gonna let more people die 'cause you can't see what he's doing is wrong!"

Suddenly the snake was flying at Andrew's face, fangs exposed, venom dripping, eyes glittering. Before Andrew had even blinked, a gun sounded and the snake dropped dead at his feet.

The rest of the snakes hissed in unison, moving forward faster than Andrew had even known snakes could move. "Mount up, boy!" Doyle shouted, holstering his gun.

Andrew scrambled onto his horse, heart pounding, and followed Charlie as he turned and headed back the way they had come. "What're we doing?" Andrew asked breathlessly.

"Goin' 'round 'em."

"Why can't we fight them?"

"They'll strike for the legs and kill the horses. Gotta go 'round."

Andrew sighed. He'd failed again. He'd failed to stop the snakes from attacking, failed to talk them around to his point of view, failed even to protect himself. I should really thank Doyle, he thought. *Don't you dare!* Why not? He saved our lives. Pecos snorted. *Take more than a puny rattlesnake bite to kill me. And we don't say "thanks". Haven't you learned nothin' yet?* Whatever.

Andrew rode for a while in silence thinking about the snakes and what the lead snake had said. Do they? he suddenly asked. *Do they what?* Animals, snakes, do they think and love? *Why wouldn't they?* They're...they're not people! Isn't that what makes people people? We think, we feel, we love, we reason. Animals don't do that. Everyone says animals don't do that. *Everyone's an idiot then!* Um...I'm not sure that makes sense.

Listen boy, there ain't much difference between you and that snake back there. Me and the owls? *Same damn thing.* But... *But what?* But...I don't get it. *I've seen coyotes with more kindness in them than man. I've seen snakes more lovin'. I've seen horses more clever.* So...what makes us better then? *Nothin'. We aint'.*

Andrew didn't know what to say to that. Maybe they weren't. Everybody said they were, but that didn't mean everybody was right. Did it? Andrew had TALKED to an owl and a snake. And a damn bear! They had spoken just like humans, but they hadn't reasoned the same, what was important wasn't the same. They were different. But not less.

Andrew frowned, feeling a little like he'd been lied to. About everything. About animals. And time travel. And magic. Everything. How could nobody know? And if they did know why were they keeping it a secret? He shook his head in frustration. This was too deep a conversation, and he had more important things to focus on right now. Like staying alive.

They rode for an hour or more, before Charlie turned east again. They switched horses often, but didn't stop for a break until sundown. Andrew brushed and fed his horses, then he sat down with the others, breathing deeply the scent of boiling coffee. He had no idea how they always managed to make a fire and get coffee boiling so fast. They just did.

"Will the snakes catch up?" Andrew asked Charlie.

Charlie closed his eyes for a long moment before replying, "No."

"But how...oh never mind. How much longer?"

"Day and a half."

Crap. He couldn't believe they'd lost so much time. "So if we ride tonight?"

"Sundown tomorrow."

"Good."

"You finally have a plan then?" the Grey Shaman asked as he sat beside Andrew.

Andrew dropped his hand from his gun with a sigh. "You've gotta stop doing that! I almost pulled my gun on you."

The Grey Shaman laughed merrily. "Pecos once shot me when I dropped in to visit."

"I can see why," Andrew snapped. "Do you seriously have nothing better to do than bug me?"

"Temper, temper. So...is your plan a good one?"

"I plan to win," Andrew said solidly.

"Ain't much of a plan," Doyle snorted.

"As far as I can tell, that's the extent of all Pecos's plans. If it's good enough for him, it'll have to be good enough for me."

The Grey Shaman laughed again. "I have always enjoyed you, Andrew."

Andrew frowned, wondering what that meant, but there was a question he needed to ask before the Grey Shaman zapped away. "You said there're many possible futures, but can you see the future? Do you know what happens? Do we win?"

"Tsk, tsk, Andrew. Wouldn't want to spoil it for yourself, would you?"

And then, just like always, he was gone. Andrew hissed in frustration. He very much would have liked to spoil it for himself. Knowing whether you won a battle was not the same as figuring out your birthday present beforehand. Knowing you won could only give you confidence. *Or maybe you wouldn't fight as hard, and then you'd lose.* But that's not how…ackk…whadda I know?

Andrew didn't want to sleep, but Charlie insisted they rest the horses for at least a couple hours, so Andrew laid his head back and closed his eyes. He wondered if this would be his last night. He wished he'd told his mom he loved her. He wished a lot of things. He wished he'd taken the trouble to learn anything other than baseball. He wished he hadn't climbed that tree. He wished he could rope.

When he finally fell asleep, his dreams were full of snakes and owls, blood and armless children, and a voice that sounded very much like his mom's asking if he wanted some lemonade.

When he woke it was still dark, and he was terrified. So terrified he couldn't even breathe. What was he thinking? This was real. All of this was real. He was going to die tomorrow. He was going to fight the enormous father of all snakes, and he was going to die.

Breathe. I can't! Andrew stumbled to his feet, tripping past the campfire, past the ever watchful eyes of Doyle, further into the dark. *Breathe, boy. In, out.* Shut up, Pecos! It's not that easy! Nothing is that easy!

Everything is "just do" for you, but it's not! I can't fight a gigantic snake and win! I CAN'T! I'm not you. I'm me! Andrew. Momma's boy! Did I tell you that?! My mom does everything for me. I'm not even sure I know how to make toast! I thought I could, but maybe I can't! I've never actually done it!

He was far enough from the campfire now that he couldn't see the glow. The moon wasn't full anymore, which meant he'd been here days, but he couldn't remember how many. Everything blurred together until it was a mass of dust and twigs and owls and bloody arms and just a mess.

"I WANNA GO HOME!!!" Andrew shouted, hoping whoever brought him heard and took pity on him. They didn't. Or if they did hear, they didn't care that he was going to die. So maybe whoever brought him wanted Pecos to die, and Andrew was just the means to the end.

Boy, listen... No, you listen, I can't do this! I can't! I'm not strong or tough! I'm not a hero! My friend bullied me into climbing a tree I didn't even wanna climb. I'm weak! Pathetic! If my mom was here, I'd run into her arms and stay there. *You ain't none of those things!* You don't even know me!!

Pecos sighed a very long sigh. *Listen up good, 'cause I'm only gonna say this once. I will not repeat myself, you hear?* Andrew nodded. *You ain't weak, you ain't pathetic, and if you are a momma's boy, who cares?* But... *I ain't finished!*

I've known grown men who complain more than you do, who can't do what you've done, who wouldn't have moved past that first bump in the road. I've known men who don't fight for nothin', not even to protect their own, but you fight for folks you don't even know. You ain't gonna die tomorrow, 'cause I ain't gonna die. We're gonna win. But how? How?! *We just will. And stop tryin' to fit your city slicker mind around that, and just do it!*

Andrew laughed out loud. He was so scared he was shaking, but somehow, somehow, he had to believe Pecos was right. He had to believe they could do this. He didn't want to die. He didn't want this to be the end. So he was going to do what Pecos said. He was going to stop thinking and "just do".

He forced air into his lungs, breathing deeply, wondering how air could smell so good. He tilted his head back and stared at the stars. They aren't this bright at home, he thought. *Really?* Really. To be honest, I've never even really noticed them, except when I'm camping, but here, they're amazing. They make the dark seem not so…dark. *I still say the heat's gone to your head a bit.* It's not my head, it's yours. *Well, never mind then. Ain't a bit of heat stupid enough to go to MY head.* Andrew grinned, thinking that was probably true.

He took one more deep breath and walked back to camp where he found the others waiting, coffee and burnt biscuits hot and ready. Andrew drank his coffee slowly, savoring it, savoring the heat, and then he stood. He was ready to ride. He was ready to fight. He was ready to win. He hoped.

He saddled Jiminty and Jeter, amazed that he could, amazed that just by feeling the buckles he knew which ones they were, and then he mounted and rode after Charlie. In less than twenty-four hours, he was going to fight Septimis, the enormous, vengeful father of all snakes. How strange that he was here now, in this time, in this place, where everything seemed too big, too bright, too beautiful, and too screwed up to be real.

Did you know your parents? he asked Pecos, thinking of his own. *Don't 'member 'em. Coyotes brought me up.* So you have coyote parents? *Had a momma. She died couple summers ago.* Sorry. *Way of life.*

Andrew missed his mom, more than he had thought he would if someone had asked. He'd missed his dad when he had first started traveling for work, but not like this, not this deep ache, this hollow hole. He honestly couldn't remember the last time he and his dad had hung out. It must have been forever ago. He hadn't realized how hard his mom had been trying to be both his mom and his dad.

She went to all his games, took him out for pizza, took him fishing and camping, tucked him in at night, cooked for him, laughed at his jokes. When he saw her again, if he saw her again, he was going to tell her thank you. *Done told you, boy. We don't say thanks.* Why not? *Makes it awkward. She's just takin' care of you. She don't expect no thanks.* Doesn't mean she doesn't deserve one. *Humph.*

Andrew tried to push thoughts of his mom away and think about Septimis and how he was going to fight him, but his mind kept drifting to the darkness. He wished he knew what it was and why it had woken Septimis. Do you think it sent the dust devils after us? *Hard to say.* Why's that? *I tend to attract trouble.* So stuff just finds you on a daily basis? *Well...not daily.* Andrew rolled his eyes.

As the sun began to rise, Andrew slowed his horse, not caring that the others moved ahead. He wanted to watch this sunrise, wanted to really enjoy it. Wanted to soak the colors into his mind and relish the way it chased the darkness away.

The sun spread across the open land, and Andrew saw part of Pecos's plan had actually worked. They were surrounded by animals. He hadn't seen them in the dark, hadn't known they were there, although he'd bet money Charlie had known. Birds flew overhead, many of them the large, black ravens, some of them hawks and eagles, some of them small, tiny birds.

There were deer and antelope and something Pecos called a mountain sheep. Andrew snickered when he saw hundreds of those prairie dog things running alongside the horses. *What?* Prairie dogs? What're they gonna do? *Just makes their courage that much greater, boy.* Andrew flushed, feeling foolish.

Far ahead he could see the outline of hundreds of coyotes, black against the rising sun, and he could feel the rush of affection Pecos felt for them. Andrew jumped when he realized there was a bear galloping beside him. There were actually a lot of bears when he looked, and a cougar or two, maybe some wolves, although Andrew wasn't sure what the difference between a wolf and a coyote was, and he definitely wasn't going to ask.

There were hundreds and hundreds of animals, and they were all headed east, towards the snake, because Andrew had asked them too, because he had told them the dust devils were somehow connected. Why do they care? he asked, knowing some would surely die and feeling awful. *Dust devils and wind witches hunt and kill, but they ain't like a cougar. They don't hunt to eat, and their hunger is never-endin'.*

Andrew cringed. That didn't sound good at all; no wonder the animals had come. He just hoped Pecos was right. He hoped Pecos was right about everything. He hoped he could win this fight, because he knew with certainty by the end of the day he'd be facing a monster.

Charlie slowed their pace, and they rode steadily through the day; animals continuing to gather, some going on ahead, some staying with them. Even the horses seemed to understand what was happening because they didn't shy when cougars or elk ran by. They just kept trotting.

Far ahead Andrew could see vultures circling in the sky. Watching them made him feel sick. He understood now what Charlie meant by "they follow death". He wished he couldn't see them; he wished he didn't know there was death up ahead.

The landscape changed again. Grass faded, replaced by large stones and huge outcroppings of rock. Scrub trees popped up around the rocks, and the ground turned an orange-red.

Andrew's heart stuttered when he heard the ground rumbling. "Is that Septimis?" he asked Charlie.

"No. Bison."

"What? Oh buffalo?"

Charlie shrugged. "They lose many to roving dust devils."

Andrew turned in his saddle and gasped when the bison ran into view. There were thousands of them. Hundreds of thousands. More; he couldn't say. There were so many they looked like a rolling sea of brown. And they were huge. The closer they got, the bigger they looked, until they were running right alongside Andrew, and the pounding of their hooves replaced the beat of his heart.

Chapter Nineteen

By late afternoon Andrew was covered in sweat, and he felt sick all over. He wanted to vomit; he wanted to crawl under a rock and hide; he wanted to run home and never leave again. He focused on breathing and asked Pecos to tell him a story. He didn't hear a word Pecos said, but Pecos's voice helped override the panic clamoring through his head.

Whadda you think'll happen if we die? Andrew asked. *I done told you, ain't gonna die.* But if we do? *Ain't. We're winnin', ain't we? I always plan to win.* Andrew rolled his eyes, but nodded. So we win. *Atta boy.*

Charlie slowed his pace, moving his horse over to Andrew. "He just went through a town," Charlie said softly.

Andrew groaned. He hadn't wanted to know, so he hadn't asked. He'd so hoped there wouldn't be any more towns; he'd hoped no one else would die. If he hadn't taken that extra time to train or that last night of rest, he could have stopped him sooner. Just another town on his head. Another town he'd been too slow and too scared to save.

"We'll catch up before he hits the next one," Charlie added. "Just another hour or so."

Andrew nodded, swallowing the bile that tried to crawl up his throat. He wasn't ready for this. He'd never be ready for this. Please send me home, he thought to whoever had brought him. Please! He closed his eyes, hoping, waiting, but when he opened them he was still looking through Pecos's eyes.

It wasn't long before Charlie halted. There was a large rise in front of them, and Andrew could hear a strange sound on the other side, like the twisting of a rusty screw. "He's on the other side," Charlie said.

"Do we just ride down there?" Andrew asked. "Like before?"

"That what Pecos wants?"

Pecos? *Well, we gotta at least try talkin' some sense into 'im. If that don't work, we fight. Leave the spares here. We'll see the layout of the land once we get on top of the ridge.*

"Leave the spares here," Andrew said. "And over the ridge we go." The others nodded. Andrew wondered what exactly it was about Pecos that made everyone so willing to follow him. Charlie, Doyle, and Joe, all the animals. Even Andrew was following him.

Andrew loosed all his horses except Dewmint, the one he was riding, and Mays, the horse carrying the rope. Then they rode over the hill, the animals trailing behind.

At the top of the hill Andrew closed his eyes and imagined himself home in bed, but when he opened them, he was still staring at Septimis rippling through the valley like a river. "He's bigger than I remembered," Andrew whispered. *Seen bigger.* You have not! *No; I really haven't. He's huge.*

Look around. What? *I wanna see the landscape.* Andrew turned left then right, slowly moving his head side to side. *I think there's a canyon just over there.* So? *Just good to know.* What else? *Nothin'. Let's ride 'bout half-way down, see if we can't get his attention.* I hate this plan. *Only plan we got.* That's why I hate it.

Andrew tried not to let his terror show as he turned to Charlie. "We're gonna ride down a ways and see if we can get his attention." Fear washed over Andrew, and he stumbled to dismount, leaning against Dewmint, breathing, trying to push it aside, but failing.

His breath came faster, and suddenly he was retching, throwing up what little food he'd eaten, making Pecos look like an idiot in front of thousands of animals. I'm sorry, Pecos, he thought, wiping his hand over his mouth. I just... Damn, I'm scared! *It'll be alright,* Pecos said softly.

Andrew didn't want to look at the others. He'd been doing so well, and he thought maybe they'd even started to like him a little, but he'd ruined it by throwing up like the sissy Pecos said he was.

He felt a hand on his shoulder and looked up to see Charlie standing beside him. "Here," Charlie said, pulling a leather cord from around his neck. "Grandmother made this. It'll help you in battle." He held the necklace out towards Andrew. "The raven feathers are for wisdom and speed; the bear tooth for strength and fierceness."

Andrew opened his mouth to speak, but he couldn't. How could Charlie be nice to him? He was puny and weak; a scared little boy. *Ain't weak, boy! You're just scared, and you'd be stupid not to be! Now put the damn necklace on, and let's get to it!*

Andrew managed a weak grin. "Thank you, Charlie," he said, slipping the necklace over his head, breathing deeply, trying to control his fear. Doyle, Charlie, and Joe were with him. They knew he was lousy at roping, they knew he wasn't Pecos, but they were still going to ride down this ridge with him and face Septimis. He mounted, tapped Dewmint in the side, and led them down the hill.

"Septimis!" he shouted when he was halfway down, and the snake's head was even with their descent. He moved slower than Andrew had remembered, massive body undulating side to side as he went.

If he heard Andrew, he didn't acknowledge it, just kept moving forward. "SEPTIMIS!" Andrew shouted again, flinching as he did, because apparently Pecos could yell really loudly.

Septimis jerked to a halt, lifting his head and swiveling around to face Andrew. "You know myyyy name?" he hissed, voice deep and rumbling.

Andrew blocked a shudder. Septimis's eyes were glittering green, his fangs were enormous and covered in thick venom, and his face was twisted in anger. "I wanna talk to you!" Andrew shouted. "You have to stop this!"

"SSStop what? Eating my fillll? Avenging the deaths of my children?! Why musssst I stop?"

"Because if you don't, I'll stop you!"

Septimis's lips twisted into a grimace which might have been a smirk and a sound like chuckling rasped past his tongue. "You and thissss tasty looking mob? I was beginning to feellll a bit hungry. That last town did not have muchhhh to offer."

"WAIT!!!!" Andrew shouted as Septimis started to move up the hill towards them. "Don't you see?! You're being used! Whatever woke you is using you!"

Septimis blinked his huge, glittering eyes, and his tongue flicked past his fangs. "And whyyyy should I care?" he hissed before rearing up to tower above them and rushing up the hill.

Crap, crap, crap! What now, Pecos? *We fight!* But how? Whadda I do? Pecos didn't get a chance to answer, because the snake was already too close, so close Andrew gasped at the size of him, the enormousness of his bulk.

"CHARGE!" Doyle yelled loudly.

The animals surged forward; rams, elk, and deer in the first line, heads lowered, horns out. The birds soared into the air as one, diving towards Septimis in a spear shape. Andrew sat on Dewmint, dumbfounded, completely at a loss at what to do.

A pack of coyotes leaped over the elk, landing on Septimis's coiling scales, ripping with their claws, tearing with their teeth, but Septimis just whipped them off. Venom dripped from his fangs, splattering on the ground, and horrible yowls and shrieks split the air. Andrew watched in horror as the venom burned straight through a coyote and into the ground.

BOY!!! Pecos yelled. Whadda I do? *FIGHT!* But…I don't know how! Andrew pulled his gun from its holster and aimed over the heads of the animals. His bullets slammed into Septimis's scales, but it was futile. Septimis didn't even bleed.

Dewmint reared as animals pushed into her, and Andrew struggled to keep his seat. He didn't have anything besides guns and knives. He watched Doyle and Joe shoot the snake's head. He saw Charlie bury arrow after arrow deep into the snake's flesh but gasped in horror as the arrows inched their way back out before dropping uselessly to the ground.

Animals ripped at his scales, but Septimis moved steadily forward, crushing them beneath his weight as he went. Andrew watched it all, wide-eyed. He'd caused this. Everyone was going to die, and it was his fault.

BOY! What?! *You gotta rope this thing. NOW!* I can't rope! *Boy, you got to. Else everyone here's gonna die!* Andrew shook himself, trying to shake off the fear holding him frozen.

Get back up the ridge. Andrew turned his horses, but in his stupor he hadn't realized Septimis had pulled his massive body around, using it to block their retreat and split the army in half.

His heart pounded. He was surrounded by animals and Septimis. How could he get to the ridge? He had to get to the ridge. He glanced around. Doyle, Charlie, and Joe had all dismounted, and they looked like tiny toy men in comparison to the gigantic snake. It wouldn't take anything for Septimis to crush them to death.

BOY!!!!! Andrew tried to force Dewmint through the animals surrounding them, but she couldn't budge. He jumped from his saddle, pushing aside a charging bear, and ripped the Stone Rope from Mays' saddle, throwing it over his shoulder.

An elk charged past him, and Andrew almost fell, but caught himself and turned towards the ridge pushing his way forward. *FASTER!* I can't! The animals were too thick, surging to move forward, surging to protect their families, surging to die. He had to save them.

"Move!" he yelled. But they didn't hear him. Every second he wasted was a second Doyle, Joe, and Charlie were in danger, and he didn't want them to be in danger. He didn't want them to die. He wedged his shoulder between a pair of rams and shoved past.

RUN! I can't! *DO IT!* Andrew braced his feet on the ground, pointing his shoulder out, and pushed off, bowling through the animals, knocking them back, ignoring the pounding pain, pushing forward and forward until he eventually reached the gigantic wall of snake.

What now? Andrew asked in panic. He hadn't realized just how big Septimis was. *JUMP!* What?! *JUMP!* That's like…it's too high! *JUST DO IT!!!* Andrew frowned. He didn't see how he could jump over something taller than a house even if he was in Pecos's body, but he didn't have a lot of options, so he may as well try.

He backed up several feet, pushing animals out of his way, and stared at the huge wall of snake in front of him. An unearthly howl sounded behind him, and Andrew flinched. He had to do this. He closed his eyes, staring at all the liquid power inside Pecos, all the strength, all the just do. Please, he said. Please help me.

Andrew ran towards the snake, getting closer and closer, and jumped, flying through the air for just a second before he slammed into a hard wall of snake flesh. He started to fall but snatched his knife, thrusting it between two scales and struggling to pull himself upwards. Septimis twitched, and Andrew flew backwards, crashing into a group of prairie dogs.

Pain slammed through Andrew's body and he fought to catch his breath as he rolled to his feet, dodging a leaping bobcat. He ran forward again, begging the strength to make him Pecos. About ten feet away, he closed his eyes because he didn't think he could do it if he saw what he was trying to do. It was impossible, he knew it was, but if he didn't look, maybe, just maybe he could do it.

He imagined himself on the other side, and he felt the power surge through him. He pushed forward, running as fast as he could, guessing when to jump, pushing off the ground so hard it hurt his feet. He felt his body lift, felt the air rush past his face, opened his eyes to see the green and orange scales of the snake pass beneath the tips of his boots, then landed with a crash on the other side in the middle of a group of bison.

I can't believe I did that, he thought as he scrambled to his feet. The top of the ridge was still so far away, and thousands of bison were between him and it. He glanced around, looking for a way through. Um…Pecos? You ever ridden a bison?

Andrew didn't wait for a reply, just grabbed the nearest bison's horns and stared into its huge brown eyes. "I need to get to the top of the ridge. Can you take me?"

To his surprise, the bison nodded. Andrew quickly grabbed a clump of shaggy fur and pulled himself onto its back, gripping tightly. The bison bellowed loudly, and the herd split in half as the bison thundered through carrying Andrew to the top of the hill.

"Thanks," Andrew gasped, dropping to the ground and turning to face the snake. He was taller than Septimis now, but only by a little bit. He dropped the Stone Rope to the ground and started to unravel it. His heart pumped madly. If only it had been anything else. Anything but a rope.

He grasped the rope right beneath the loop, feeling the smoothness of it in his hands. He wished it was rough like Pecos's rope. He should have practiced with the Stone Rope. He'd just been scared, scared he wouldn't be able to spin it.

He held his breath, trying to feel every bit of Pecos's power, trying to let it infuse him, to wash away Andrew and leave only Pecos. He closed his eyes, hoping, and started spinning. *You're doin' it, boy!* Andrew's eyes snapped open. He was doing it! The rope was spinning high above him. *Bit faster.* Andrew sped it up, waiting for the right moment, trying to forget about the rope and focus on Septimis. He fumbled slightly when he saw Septimis strike at Charlie, but Charlie leaped backwards, and the snake hit empty ground.

When he rears back up, release. Andrew stilled his breathing, focusing on the rush of the air around his face, watching Septimis, waiting. The snake raised his head high above the others, eyes glinting, fangs gleaming in the low sun, and Andrew loosed the rope.

It flew through the air, over the valley, straight towards Septimis, glittering as the sun glanced off its golden strands. Andrew held his breath, then hissed in dismay as the rope flew past Septimis's head, landing just on the other side of his body.

"Crap!" Andrew yelled, fumbling at the rope to pull it back in. Septimis stilled, noticing the rope, eyes following its gleaming strands up the ridge to Andrew. His eyes narrowed, and his tongue flickered.

"Double crap," Andrew hissed, pulling the rope faster and faster.

"I had missstaken you for the renowned warrior I was told about, but youuu are not heeee, are you?" Septimis hissed loudly, curling his body around, crushing hundreds of animals as he went.

Andrew screamed, ripping the rope with all his might, snatching the loop from the air, and struggling to get it spinning again. He spun the rope faster and faster, watching in horror as Septimis ignored the animals attacking him and focused solely on Andrew. Andrew breathed out, imagining the rope settling over

Septimis's head, holding him still, giving all the animals time to move away while Andrew figured out how to beat him to death.

NOW! Andrew stared at Septimis's head and let the rope fly. It sailed beautifully through the air, landing right in front of Septimis.

Septimis chuckled deeply. "You cannot ropeeee. How very frussssstrating that must be."

Andrew's hands were shaking, his whole body was shaking, but he jerked on the rope, pulling it back in again, ripping it through the bison. "MOVE!" he yelled. "GET OUT OF THE WAY!!! HE'LL CRUSH YOU!" He couldn't fail again; he only had one more chance, one last shot.

Somehow the rope was in the air again, spinning like mad. Dust whirled around Andrew, but all he could see was Septimis. All he could see was Septimis's eyes. His glittering eyes. *What you doin', boy?,* he heard Pecos snap, but Pecos's voice was distant, far away. What was he doing? Why was he here? Andrew couldn't remember. He felt the rope slip through his fingers, but he didn't care. All the fear was gone, replaced by a strange sort of weightlessness. He was floating.

An angry yell shattered the silence around him, and suddenly Andrew was free. He blinked rapidly. What had just happened? What the hell was he doing? The Stone Rope lay on the ground at his feet, and he scrambled for it, grabbing it, spinning it into the air once more.

He gasped when he saw Doyle ripping at Septimis's back, tearing away at it with his knife. Septimis jerked sideways, trying to dislodge Doyle, hissing angrily. Andrew bit his lip and kept spinning. The only way he could help Doyle was by throwing the damn rope!

Septimis reared, pitching Doyle backwards, and Andrew flinched as Doyle landed with a crash against a huge rock. He spun the rope faster and higher, ignoring Septimis when he turned back towards Andrew, slithering closer and closer.

The rope was spinning beautifully, and Andrew knew this was it. His last chance. He stared at Septimis, terrified to let go, knowing he would miss. *Let me do it,* Pecos said softly.

Andrew's heart stopped as he felt a huge, warm hand slip over his own and suddenly the rope was gone! Flying through the air, humming as it went, singing through the sunlight. He held his breath, hoping. The rope flew up and up and when it finally came down, it came down around Septimis's head, slipping past his snarling mouth and settling around his enormous throat.

"YOU DID IT!" Andrew shouted, jerking the rope tight and jumping up and down. "You did it!" *We did it. Now let's see what this rope can do!*

Chapter Twenty

Septimis reared back, struggling to jerk the rope from Andrew's hands, but Andrew held strong. The rope ripped and burned, but Andrew didn't let go.

Septimis's eyes narrowed angrily. "SSSStupid human! Nothing can hold meeee!"

He ripped backwards, pulling Andrew towards the edge of the ridge. Pecos! It's not working! *I see that. New plan.* What's that? *I'm thinkin'.* Think faster, Andrew growled, digging his feet into the ground and fighting to hold Septimis still.

"PECOS!" Andrew screamed, flying into the air as Septimis ripped backwards again. Andrew jerked hard, wrapping the rope around his hands, yanking with his whole body, begging Pecos's strength to help him. When his feet touched the ground again, he pulled with all his might, trying desperately to hold the monster in place.

The canyon! The what? *The canyon. Force 'im into the canyon; fall might at least knock 'im out.* And how do I do that? *Ride 'im.* I'm sorry, did you say "ride him"? *Yep.* "Worst plan ever," Andrew ground out.

Septimis jerked again, but this time Andrew didn't fight him. Instead he pushed off the ground, soaring through the air towards Septimis and landing with a thump on Septimis's chest. His scales were slick, and

Andrew started sliding down. He scrambled with his feet, holding the rope in one hand and ripping his knife from its sheath with his other, stabbing it deep into Septimis's body.

Septimis hissed angrily, glaring down at Andrew. Andrew ripped his knife free and swung around the side to avoid a stream of venom. He swung all the way around to Septimis's back, then used his knife to climb higher.

Septimis hissed loudly, shaking side to side, trying to dislodge Andrew, but Andrew slowly made his way up to where the rope had settled around the snake's neck. Andrew pulled the rope as tightly as possible, cutting off the blood to his hand, trying to choke Septimis out, anything to make him stop thrashing around.

"Youuu cannot stop meeee!" Septimis hissed angrily. "I seeeee now that you are nothing but a childdd! I have been alive since the beginning! I willlll crush you! I willlll crush your army! I WILLLLL CRUSH YOUR ENTIRE RACE!!!"

Andrew stabbed his knife into the back of Septimis's neck as far as he could. He ripped it out and stabbed again and again. But every time Septimis's flesh resealed itself. He's invincible! Andrew thought, feeling pure terror. *Nothing's invincible, boy. Just gotta find the right spot.* Where the hell is it?! *Not sure yet.* Damn it, Pecos!

Andrew ripped on the rope, trying to steer Septimis toward the canyon lip, but he wouldn't budge, just continued to buck and fight. Whadda I do? Andrew asked, full of dread. *Try beatin' his head in.* Andrew tried to climb higher, but Septimis thrashed so wildly, Andrew couldn't do anything more than hang on.

He glanced down, hoping the others had moved and were safe. He saw Charlie and Joe on top of the ridge, animals gathered around them, but he couldn't see Doyle. "Damn it," he growled. "If you killed Doyle..." He didn't finish, couldn't finish. Doyle wasn't dead. He couldn't be. He was too mean to die.

There were dead animals spread across the plain beneath him, and vultures were circling in the sky, waiting. Andrew hated them. He had to kill Septimis. He had to. He had to kill him for all the animals that had already died, all the people who had died, he had to do it for Pecos, he had to do it for Doyle, he had to do it for himself.

He grinned, suddenly realizing that even though he couldn't steer Septimis, he could keep him from striking. "BISON!!!!" he shouted loudly, hoping they could hear him over Septimis's thrashing and hissing. "I NEED YOU!!!" He saw them lift their heads, one after another, until the entire herd of bison was staring at him, waiting to hear what he said. "PUSH HIM INTO THE CANYON!" he screamed.

The bison lowered their heads as one and rushed forward, slamming into Septimis's side with such force, Andrew had to tighten his grip to keep from falling. Septimis snarled in rage, raising his head to strike, but Andrew braced his feet against Septimis's neck and held him back with the rope.

"I will eat you alllll!" Septimis cried as the bison rammed into him again and again. "I willlll eat your childrennn! I will wipe you frommm the face of the earth!" The bison were hitting in waves, one group after the other, not giving Septimis any time to slither away.

Even with Pecos's power rushing through him, Andrew was tiring. His hands were bleeding, his head hurt horribly, and his vision was bleary, but he couldn't stop. He wrapped the rope around his arm, refusing to give up, refusing to let go, refusing to let Septimis win. The bison rammed into the snake again and again, shaking the ground so hard Andrew could feel it.

Septimis fought so fiercely Andrew couldn't keep his feet braced, but he used the full weight of his body and all of Pecos's strength to keep Septimis's head upright and away from the bison.

They were close to the canyon now; so close Andrew could see into it. It was a very long way to the bottom. He didn't know for sure if it would hurt Septimis to fall so far, but he knew without a doubt it would hurt him.

"Go big or go home," he whispered, ignoring the blood running down his arms and tightening his grip once more.

Septimis ripped sideways, and Andrew fell against the snake's side, flinching as he hit, feeling as if he'd slammed into solid rock. He glanced under his hands and saw the scales were fading, turning grey. What's happening, Pecos? *Oh...the STONE ROPE.* What?

The grey was spreading, running down Septimis's body and up over his head. He was turning to stone, just like the warrior from the story. Pure relief rushed through Andrew. They had won! "We did it, Pecos!" he exclaimed. "We did it!"

He didn't have time to say or think anything else because at that instant the bison hit again and Septimis tumbled over the edge of the canyon taking Andrew with him.

Joe watched in shock as the entire snake careened over the side of the canyon. He couldn't see much past the thousands of bison, but he was certain Pecos went with it. He pushed past the animals in front of him and started running. Suddenly there was a thunderous crash, and the ground shook violently, knocking him to the ground.

Dust and stones rained from the sky, but Joe scrambled to his feet, ignoring the pelting rocks, pushing past the huge bison, and running the rest of the way to the canyon lip. He stumbled when he reached the edge, skidding to a stop, and gazed down into the gorge, feeling sick. There was no way anyone could have survived that fall. Not even Pecos.

"Where is he?" Doyle gasped, limping up behind Joe.

Joe shook his head. "He…he went over with it."

"Charlie," Doyle snapped. "Is he down there? Is he alive?"

"There's no one," Charlie said softly, joining them. "I see nothing."

"Damn it!" Doyle yelled. "Take more than a fall like that to kill Pecos! You know that!"

"But the boy..." Joe started to say.

"The boy..." Doyle whispered, stepping closer to the edge and staring down. "I can't... believe it." Silence spread across the valley and canyon as the stones stopped raining and the dust began to settle.

"Hey guys!" Andrew shouted, dropping to the ground behind them. "Did you see that?! We did it!"

They jerked, turning around so quickly Doyle almost slipped over the edge, but Charlie grabbed him by the arm, pulling him back.

"We thought...you..." Joe didn't finish.

"Oh! Sorry. No. I caught a ride. Didn't you see?" Andrew pointed above him where several huge ravens were flying swiftly into the sunset. "They grabbed me just before Septimis hit the bottom."

"Sorry," Andrew said again when no one said anything. He grinned happily at Doyle. "I'm glad you're alright; I thought maybe...anyway. Pecos says you should know better than to think something as tiny as that snake would be the end of him."

Joe laughed loudly and slapped Andrew on the back. Charlie grinned, but Doyle just grunted. Andrew looked around sadly. Most of the animals were already far away, walking, running, or flying back to their lives. But so many lay dead. There were so many dead he couldn't even count them. He looked for the bison, but they had already disappeared.

"I didn't get a chance to thank them," he said softly. *Boy...* I know, I know; we don't say thanks. "Now what?" Andrew asked.

"Now what, what?" replied Joe.

"We won. Whadda we do now?" Andrew still couldn't believe they had actually won. He'd been certain they were going to die there for a moment.

"Go back to the ranch."

"Oh." But what about the dark? Don't we need to hunt it down? It's clearly up to no good. Andrew shivered, remembering his dreams. Never mind. The ranch sounds good. Let's go there. *Sure,* Pecos agreed.

The sun was setting behind the hills casting a dark shadow over the bodies of the dead animals. Suddenly the shadow grew darker, so dark, it gave Andrew chills. The shadow stretched and stretched, growing until it covered the entire valley, filling it with blackness and icy cold, then the sun burst through with one last splendid ray, chasing the shadow away.

Andrew's face paled, and his blood turned cold. Pecos? *I see it, boy.* What happened? *Don't know.* The bodies of all the animals were gone, stripped, and in their place was nothing but bones; gleaming, white bones.

Andrew closed his eyes, not believing it, too frightened to believe it, and when he opened them again he was looking across his room at his window.

"What!" he gasped. "Pecos?" There was no answer. Andrew closed his eyes again, but when he opened them he was still him.

He felt his face; it was smooth, not covered in rough whiskers. He stared at his hands; they seemed pale and small, but they were his. He was back in his own body! He was home. For a second he felt such utter relief he could barely breathe, and then he just stared at his hands in wonder. How he had missed them!

But how? What had happened? Had it been a dream after all? He couldn't believe that. It hadn't been. It was real. He knew it was real. He struggled to sit up straighter, then froze, heart skipping a beat. Sitting on his lap were three things that hadn't been there before, couldn't have been there before, shouldn't be there now. Doyle's carving, Joe's watch, and Charlie's necklace.

Andrew raised a trembling hand to touch them, half expecting them to disappear, not believing they were really there. His finger brushed the smooth wood of the raven's wings, and he jerked his hand back, gasping. How?

He stared around his room; everything looked exactly the same. The sun was still shining outside his window. The painted stars still covered his ceiling. His leg was still encased in a red cast, and the book of American lore was sitting half-open on his lap.

He carefully picked up Joe's watch, flipping the cover open and reading the inscription, hearing Joe's voice in his mind, telling him it would remind him of whatever he needed to remember. The second hand was still moving, and a quick glance at his alarm clock told him the time was correct. He frowned in confusion, tracing a finger gently over one of the raven feathers on Charlie's necklace, remembering Charlie's sly grin and lilting words. He held the raven carving in the palm of his hand, remembering how Doyle was angry and gruff, but secretly patient.

Pecos? he thought. Nothing. No gruff "what, boy?", no chuckle, no "humph". Nothing but Andrew's own thoughts, his own confusion, his own mind. He missed him. How could he miss him? He missed them all. He'd only just met them, but he felt as if they'd been part of his life forever. He felt as if the world was suddenly dimmer, darker, less amazing.

He swiped a tear from his eye and picked up the book. Had it somehow sent him? He read the copyright page with a frown. The copyright date was listed as "Sometime". What did that even mean? Andrew was so confused. He read the cover again, taking note of the author's name, G. A. Oldman. The name sent a shiver down his spine, but he didn't know why.

He flipped to chapter one and started to read the story again. It was a story about the time Pecos had roped a tornado, and Pecos had told Andrew that story, and the book hadn't gotten it right.

Andrew read all the way through to the end, but nothing happened. Pecos didn't appear, and Andrew didn't go there. The story just ended. Pecos rode off into the sunset, but Andrew stayed in his room. He flipped through the rest of the book, but the other chapters weren't about Pecos. Andrew didn't care about Johnny Appleseed or Paul Bunyan. But what if it wasn't about Pecos? What if it was about something else?

Andrew frowned and started to read the chapter about John Henry. Nothing happened. He looked at the book with narrowed eyes and bent to sniff it once more; there was something vaguely familiar about that tobacco smell, besides Grandpa Lester.

"Andrew? Do you want some lemonade?"

Andrew jumped sideways, reaching for a gun that wasn't there, before he realized his mom had just walked into his room. "You scared me!" he gasped.

"I'm sorry. I called from downstairs a couple minutes ago."

"You did?" Andrew suddenly remembered his dream, the one where he'd heard his mom asking if he wanted lemonade. He blinked rapidly. "How long has it been since you last came up?"

"I don't know. Thirty minutes or so."

Andrew wrapped his fingers around Doyle's carving, needing to feel it, needing to know it hadn't been a dream; it had been real; it had been real.

He stared at his mom, feeling like he hadn't seen her in years. He struggled to stand and hugged her tightly. He'd thought he would never see her again. Never hear her voice again. He hadn't known how much he would miss her.

She hugged him back, then tilted her head and stared at him. "You okay, baby?" she asked with a concerned smile.

Andrew grinned. "Yeah. I'm sorry I was mean earlier. I'm just...upset is all. Thanks." He paused, flopping back down on his bed. "You're an awesome mom." Pecos might not approve, but Andrew needed to say it.

Tears gathered in Mrs. Rufus's eyes, and she leaned forward to hug him again. "Thank you, baby. I'm so sorry; I know this is hard on you. I'll call Chuck's dad when they get home from camping and ask him to move you downstairs."

"It's okay, Mom," Andrew said, patting her awkwardly on the back. "I'm fine up here."

"Is there anything you need?" she asked, rubbing her hand over his hair.

"What about a cup of coffee?" he asked, suddenly wanting coffee more than anything else in the world.

"Coffee?" She laughed loudly. "Not gonna happen, kid. How about some cocoa?"

"Okay," Andrew agreed with a sigh. "Thanks."

She left the room chuckling, leaving Andrew alone with his thoughts. He tried to count how many days he'd been gone, but everything kind of blurred together. He thought it had been about two weeks, give or take.

He shuddered, suddenly realizing it had been two whole weeks since he'd brushed his teeth or taken a shower, never mind that he'd been in Pecos's body. He hadn't noticed at the time, and he honestly hadn't felt dirty, but now he felt disgusting, like he must be coated in two weeks' worth of sweat and blood.

He hobbled to his window. The air felt stiff and lifeless in his room, so he pushed the window open, removed the screen, and leaned his head outside, taking a deep breath of air. It wasn't nearly as fresh as Pecos's air, but it was air.

He couldn't figure out what had happened, not really. Someone or something had sent him back in time, putting him in Pecos's body. Pecos was real, not just a legend. Well, he was a legend, just a real legend.

Andrew frowned, thinking it out. Someone wanted Pecos dead. But if that was the case, why had they sent Andrew back home after he and Pecos had defeated Septimis? Why not leave him there? Given enough time, Andrew was sure he could have accidentally killed them both. It was all so confusing.

He closed his eyes and ran through it all in his mind. He remembered the pain, the absolute terror. He felt the anguish and weight of his failure. He basked in that moment, the moment when they had won, triumphed, conquered evil. He remembered how elated he'd felt, how relieved.

And then he remembered plummeting over the edge of the canyon into nothingness. He held his breath, feeling the air rush past him, feeling the weightlessness. There was no time to think, to wonder what it would feel like when he hit the bottom.

Good ride, boy, Pecos had said right before they hit the bottom. But they never did.

They had flown, flown right out of the canyon, rocks and dirt raining all around them. It had been absolutely incredible! The ravens had saved them. Andrew wished he'd been able to tell them thank you. He grinned, knowing how much Pecos would hate that.

But why? Why had he been sent? Why had he been pulled back? And at that exact moment? It didn't make sense. And the shadow? What the hell was the shadow? Was it the darkness?

He spent the entire afternoon chasing thoughts through holes in his mind, but getting nowhere. He refused any more pain pills, just on principal, but ate all the food his mom offered him, feeling like he hadn't eaten real food in months.

That night, he struggled to fall asleep. He missed Joe's music, the crackling of the fire, the breeze on his face, and the stars up above. His neon stars seemed a ludicrous imitation. When he finally fell asleep, he dreamed of a dark shadow eating the flesh of broken children. He woke feeling nauseous. Whatever had happened, whatever the reason, why ever he'd been sent, it wasn't over. Not by a long shot.

"Mom," he asked when Mrs. Rufus brought him breakfast, which Andrew was happy to see did not include burnt biscuits. "Do you think you could go to the library again?"

"Don't you like the books I got you?"

"Oh, no, it's not that. I just thought of some other books I'd like."

"Sure, what do you want?"

"Any books on history, 1865 or so, American West, anything about Pecos Bill, magic, time travel, shamans, snakes, ravens, or American Indian Mythology, cowboys and cattle drives!"

His eyes glowed as he spoke. He might be gone, but he wasn't done. He was going to find Pecos. He was going to find a way to get back or a way to talk to Pecos or see him one last time. Andrew had to know what the dark was, had to know who had sent him, had to know what happened next.

Epilogue

"What do you think you are doing?! You almost got Pecos killed!"

"Ah, but I didn't, did I?" Grey replied lazily, smoking his pipe.

"And what would you have done if you had?"

"Tried again."

"Tried again?! You cannot! Time is too delicate! What game are you playing?"

"It is not a game, sister mine."

"It is always a game to you. Meddling, moving things about to suit your mood. You cannot. I will not allow you to hurt him."

"Even you sister, cannot stand in my way." And then, just so he didn't have to hear her continue to rant, Grey disappeared and left White all alone, standing in his empty cabin, smoke drifting through the air.

Somewhere else, far away, in the shifting dark of night, the voice of darkness seethed with anger. It had been so close, so close. Now it had to begin again, begin anew. But it would. It was nothing if not patient. Very, very patient...

The End

Book 2: BONE DEEP

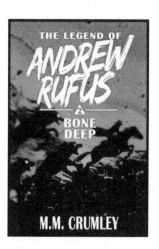

Excerpt

Andrew stood in the middle of an open plain, surrounded by death. Burned, maimed bodies littered the charred ground, crumpled at his feet, all around him. Horrific cries of agony filled the air, piercing his ears, hurting his head. The stench of death and ash was unbearable. Cinder wolves lined the horizon, howling. Rolling black smoke poured off them, filling the sky. His heart pounded madly. Where was he? What had happened?

"PECOS!" he screamed. "Where are you?"

He turned in a circle and gasped. A man was sprawled across the ground beside Andrew, half his face burned to the bone, body covered in blood. Andrew dropped beside him, grabbing his wrist, feeling for a pulse. Feeling nothing. He was dead.

"Everyone is dead," a silky voice purred. "Pecos cannot save you; he is weak. You will die. But I can save you. I can free you. Would you like to be free?"

"Who are you?" Andrew cried. "Where are you?"

"I am here. Where is Pecos? Hiding!"

Andrew shook his head. "Pecos doesn't hide. He fights!"

"Then where is he?"

"I don't know," Andrew whimpered, burying his face in his hands. How had this happened? How could everyone be dead?

"Let Pecos die, and I will save you."

Andrew's head jerked up. "What?!"

Part of the black cloud swirled around Andrew, morphing into a tall, willowy, faceless form. A freezing cold, black tendril reached out, brushing a tear from Andrew's cheek. Andrew ripped away, hating the cold of it.

"Let Pecos die, little boy. Just let him die."

"No! I can't do that!"

"You can; he cannot stop you," the voice crooned. "Just let the wolves have him."

Andrew stumbled to his feet, facing the voice, heart pounding, body quacking. "NO!"

"Then you will die! And if you die, Pecos will die anyway!"

"I don't care! If you could kill me you'd've already done it. Whatever you are, Pecos and I are gonna hunt you down and kill you!" Andrew ground out.

The cloud changed into a brutal wind, knocking Andrew back, stealing his breath. "Stupid boy!" the voice raged. "You will suffer; you will both suffer, and I will suck the life from your bones!"

ORDER TODAY AT AMAZON.COM

A Note to My Readers:

Thank you so much for reading DARK AWAKENING. I hope you enjoyed it as much as I did. I wanted to make mention that although I spent a lot of time doing historical research while writing the story of Andrew and Pecos, their story is in no way intended to be a historical novel or even an accurate representation of the times. Many of the details are garnered from history, but those of you who are well-versed in the late 1860's may notice a few slight discrepancies. However since this is a work of fiction and not a historical novel, I allowed my characters to lead the way, changing what needed to be changed, preserving what could be preserved, and letting them tell their story in their own words.

Some of my characters, such as Charlie, Grandma, and the Grey Shaman, are Native American; however, you will notice I did not name any tribes or specific people. There are so many wonderful and unique Native American tribes I don't feel I could possibly represent one specific culture accurately. I wanted to include Native American characters, in fact, the story would not work without them, but I didn't want to unintentionally misrepresent a culture.

My Best Regards,

M. M. Crumley

Made in the USA
Coppell, TX
03 December 2020